Bradley dashed from the room before Melissa finished her sentence and returned within three minutes. He dumped his entire lunch in the garbage pail except for his empty thermos, then sat at his desk. "Uncle Josh is coming," he said with a big smile that extended nearly ear to ear. "My Uncle Josh is really nice. Do you think Uncle Josh is nice?"

"Yes, your uncle is very nice."

"Uncle Josh makes good spaghetti. He even made pizza once."

"Uncle Josh sounds like a good cook."

"Yes, he is. He's good at fixing cars too." Bradley's smile widened as he sat at his desk, not moving a muscle. He folded his hands on the desk in front of him, straightened his back, and planted his feet firmly on the floor while he waited very patiently, especially for a six year old.

Melissa checked her watch a number of times as everyone else in the room ate their lunches while Bradley continued to sit as still as a statue. Melissa wondered how she could get the entire class to sit like that at the same time, even for a few minutes.

GAIL SATTLER lives in Vancouver, BC (where you don't have to shovel rain) with her husband, three sons, dog, and countless fish, many of which have names. She writes inspirational romance because she loves happily-ever-afters and believes God has a place in that happy ending. Visit Gail's website at http://www.gailsattler.com.

HEARTSONG PRESENTS

McMillian's Matchmakers

Gail Sattler

Heartsong Presents

A note from the author:
I love to hear from my readers! You may correspond with me
by writing:

> **Gail Sattler**
> **Author Relations**
> **PO Box 719**
> **Uhrichsville, OH 44683**

ISBN 1-58660-378-7

MCMILLIAN'S MATCHMAKERS

Cover design by Jocelyne Bouchard.

PRINTED IN THE U.S.A.

prologue

"I don't know how I'll ever repay you for this, Josh."

Josh McMillian studied his brother. He couldn't imagine the torment that had brought Brian to this decision. Once more, he read the piece of paper in his hand in an effort to let what the magnitude of what he'd just agreed to do sink in.

He cleared his throat. "Don't worry. Everything will be fine."

"I'm going to ask you one more time. I know the papers have been signed, and everything is all binding and legal, but it's not too late to reverse it. Are you sure you want to do this? It's a big responsibility."

What he wanted to do and what he needed to do were two completely different things. The future of not only his brother and sister-in-law but also his nephews now rested with him and his decision. He couldn't say no. They were all the family he had, and they needed him.

Josh stiffened and cleared his throat. "Yes, I'm sure. And I'm going to ask you one more time too. Are you sure you're okay with this?"

Brian's eyes watered, and his voice cracked when he finally spoke. "Yes. That clinic in Switzerland is the only hope we've got left. I have no choice. I've got to take her. Without the kids."

"You know I'll be praying for Sasha. And you too."

His brother acknowledged his promise with a nod. "The treatment might take years, you know."

"I know that."

Brian extended his hand, and Josh met his handshake.

Tears flowed down his brother's cheeks, as he gave Josh's hand a firm squeeze. "I'll see you at the airport tomorrow, and then that's it."

"Yes. That's it."

With those words, Josh knew his life would never be the same again.

one

"Why are my socks pink? I'm not wearing pink socks to school."

"Help! Help! The toilet is spilling!"

"Who ate the last apple? That was for my lunch, and it's gone."

"It didn't have your name on it."

"That's my shirt. You can't wear my shirt. Take it off!"

"Hey, you guys! Be quiet! I'm on the phone!"

"Uncle Josh! Tell Ryan it's my shirt!"

"I can't get my science project wet, and it's raining. I have to be at school early today to set it up. I need a ride, Uncle Josh."

Josh stared in silence into his coffee cup, badly needing that first sip, but he thought the overflowing toilet probably should be his first priority.

Fortunately, he hadn't had time to put on his own socks yet, so all that got wet were his bare feet when he reached behind the toilet to turn off the water. He said a silent prayer of thanks that not much water had overflowed, while he shooed Bradley out of the bathroom to split up the fight between Ryan and Kyle. He quickly sent Tyler to find the plunger while he wiped up the water with the dog's towel.

"Where's Andrew?" he called out, as he threw the dirty towel into the bathtub.

"I'm here, Uncle Josh."

"Pack that science project in the van. I'll be out as soon as I can."

"All right!" Andrew jumped up, made a fist in the air, and pulled it down in triumph.

"How come he's getting a ride? I want a ride too."

Ryan appeared and started tugging on his shirt. "Me too! Me toooo!"

Tyler hung up the phone. "Can we give Allyson a ride? She can't find her umbrella."

Josh ran into his bedroom to find his last clean pair of socks, which fortunately were black, not pink like Kyle's. Hopefully the rest of whatever else was in the washing machine last night wasn't also pink, although he now had a feeling he knew where Bradley's favorite new red shirt went.

"I guess so, Tyler. We've got seven seats, no sense in leaving one empty, especially first thing in the morning." He noticed that Tyler didn't pick up on his intended sarcasm, but then, Josh didn't know if he would have understood adult sarcasm when he was fifteen, either.

Josh turned to Ryan and Kyle and Bradley, who were still fighting over shirts and apples. "Everybody grab your lunches, and I'll drive you all if we leave now. Just make sure you brush your teeth first."

The mad scramble and squabbling over the toothpaste answered his question about who hadn't yet brushed their teeth.

"Come on, you guys. I can't be late for work again. Get moving."

He waited for everyone in the minivan, then began the round-trip of picking up Tyler's friend and delivering all of them to their respective schools on time. When the van was finally quiet and empty, he made a quick stop at the house to grab his own lunch, which he'd forgotten in the rush, and continued on his way to work, hoping he could make it without being late after adding the unexpected delay.

He pulled into his parking space at the shop and ran into the building with one minute to spare—without a speeding ticket.

Before he accepted legal guardianship of his five nephews, he was fifteen minutes early every day. Because he now required six seats, he put his sports car into storage and started driving his brother's minivan. Not that he had a very active social life before, but up until he started living with his nephews, he actually had time to date. He'd even thought he and Theresa had been getting pretty serious. Now, the only women he had seen lately were the sitter and the mothers of the other kids on the soccer team, all of whom were married and older than him by five or more years.

"Good thing you made it here early, McMillian. Busy lineup today."

Josh checked the board for the schedule as he stepped into his coveralls, which were clean and pressed. He wondered if the company that laundered the auto shop's coveralls also did residential jobs.

According to the list, it looked like any other day, full of tune-ups—a few transmission problems, some complaints about cars making strange noises, and a bit of warranty work. "I don't see anything out of the ordinary here, Rick. You hiding something?"

"Mrs. Kabelevsky bought a car for her grandson, and she wants it running perfect. Right there in stall three."

Josh cringed and ran his fingers through his hair when he recognized the old car. "She was in here yesterday with that thing, and I recommended against buying it because of the amount of work it needed."

His boss appeared beside him. "And she said she appreciated your honesty. That's why she bought it. Since you outlined exactly everything you saw wrong with it, she trusts you to fix it. She says it reminded her of her first car, and that's why she wanted to give this one in particular to her grandson. She said she knows you won't let her down. She's our best customer, Josh."

"Thanks for the reminder," he grumbled as they walked to the car together and raised the hood. Josh stared blankly into the engine compartment. "I told her not to buy this."

"You already said that."

"Does she have any idea how much this is going to cost? It

might be better just to get a rebuilt engine. The body isn't in great shape, either. She's going to pay more to fix it than she paid for it in the first place."

"She said money is no object."

Josh wondered if one day, when he had children of his own, and then grandchildren, if he'd ever be in a position to buy an older car and pay to have it fixed to his satisfaction.

He stopped himself from perusing that line of thought. It was never going to happen. Even though he was now twenty-five, his chances of getting married had decreased to somewhere below zero.

He'd been seriously dating Theresa for three years and was ready make their relationship permanent. Taking guardianship of his nephews required making some major adjustments to his life, but this one thing he hadn't seen coming.

Theresa liked children, but apparently not as much as he thought. Not long after he moved into his brother's house to care for his nephews, everything changed. He'd tried to tell her that even though the boys would be under his care for a few years, it probably wouldn't be permanent. But, until his brother and sister-in-law came back, he was the boys' only hope of staying together as a family. Theresa had argued that if it wasn't permanent, his brother wouldn't have gone through the proceedings of giving him legal guardianship.

He had understood that the reason for the proceedings to change the status of his relationship to the boys from merely "uncle" to legal guardianship was in case he had to make any formal decisions or other authorizations in the event of an absent parent or, heaven forbid, in case of some emergency, since Brian and Sasha would be extremely difficult to contact at the best of times and impossible to contact on short notice. However, the bottom line was that he really didn't know how long the boys would be with him. The possibility existed that Sasha would never get better, and, if not, then because of her mental state, she might never be able to be a fit parent. Brian was doing all he could to help her, participating in a very specialized treatment plan while there was still a chance that medication and rehabilitation could make her better.

Until that happened, Josh accepted the responsibility of raising five growing and active boys.

After only two weeks of his caring for his nephews, Theresa told him that she didn't want to see him again because she didn't want to date a day care. He had tried to tell her it wasn't like a day care at all. They weren't toddlers by any stretch of the imagination. The boys were 6, 8, 10, 13, and 15. The oldest, Tyler, was more than capable of baby-sitting his brothers, even though it was sometimes difficult to pin him down long enough to get a commitment out of him. He especially didn't want to press Tyler too far, because all of them felt not only the loss of their parents but also the stress of the new environment.

Josh let out a long sigh and returned his thoughts to his work, where they should have been in the first place. It was going to be a trying day, and he needed to be home on time. Tonight he had to help Tyler with a major French assignment, take Kyle to swimming lessons, and Bradley to Cub Scouts. He also had a couple of loads of laundry to do, and he had no idea what they were going to do about supper because in the scramble this morning he'd forgotten to take something out of the freezer. He also didn't know if they had enough milk for bedtime cereal, but even if they didn't, he doubted that he'd have time to go to the store before it closed. Somewhere in there, he had to try to do something about the wash load of pink socks, or else he would have to buy all the boys new socks.

In other words, today was just like any other day.

≈

Melissa Klassen checked the clock. "We only have five minutes left, class. If you haven't finished your printing, then you'll have to take it home. Everyone, please, tidy up your desks, and be quiet and courteous to everyone around you."

She put on her best teacher smile on the outside, but on the inside, smiling was the last thing she felt like doing. After a hectic day she was more than just tired; she was completely exhausted.

Tomorrow was the school's science fair, and, as usual, the grade one students' plans and dreams for their projects far exceeded their abilities. While many of the children were rightly proud of their accomplishments, others were sadly disappointed with their finished projects, all of which were now on display in the school gymnasium ready for tomorrow's judging.

Today she'd had to deal with frustration, disappointment, tears, and one very unpleasant incident that in the adult world would have been called "road rage." In her class of six and seven year olds, Melissa called it a temper tantrum. For the first time in so long that she couldn't remember when, she needed to go straight home and have a nap. Tonight was the monthly Sunday school teachers meeting, and they usually ran late into the evening. She needed to be alert to participate in the agenda planning.

"Miss Klassen? Can I go to the bathroom?"

Again, she looked up at the clock. She no longer had the energy to correct the child that the proper word in the context of the question was "may." "The bell will ring in one minute, Caroline. Can you wait for one minute?"

The little girl squirmed in her chair. "Nooo."

Melissa squeezed her eyes shut for a brief second. "Yes, you may go."

The bell rang ten seconds after Caroline closed the door behind her.

"Class dismissed. Remember to push your chairs in, and go get your jackets and backpacks quietly. I'll see you all again tomorrow."

The room was quiet except for the shuffling of little feet for about five seconds before the energy of the class ignited into an uproar.

She didn't have the strength to try to calm them. Besides, in four minutes they'd all be gone. It wasn't worth the effort.

She waited for Caroline to return from the bathroom to claim her sweater and backpack, and then, except for the echoed noise of the clamoring in the hall, her classroom was quiet.

Melissa surveyed the room. Everything was relatively uncluttered, especially considering that today the children had completed the finishing touches to their science projects, which had been a month in the making.

As she walked between the desks to push the chairs in properly for the custodian and tidy up some of the stray messes, she lingered at Bradley McMillian's desk, then closed her eyes to say a brief prayer for him.

Little Bradley had more than his share of worries. She wasn't aware of the exact details of the situation, nor was it her place to know them. A month ago she had been advised by the office that his parents had left the country indefinitely, and Bradley and his four brothers had been left in the care of their uncle, who was now their legal guardian.

Although understandable and expected, the changes in Bradley's behavior gave her cause for concern. Unlike before his parents left, he now often paid inordinate amounts of attention to fine detail in his printing and drawing. Other days she caught him with his work almost untouched while he stared blankly out the window, lost in his own world of thought. Her heart went out to him. Whatever the circumstances, even if it were not the case, any child would feel abandonment with his parents suddenly gone, and she worried about the effect of such thoughts, however misplaced. The heart of a child was a fragile thing.

After a few moments, Melissa continued to walk around the classroom to push in the rest of the chairs, then slipped on her jacket, picked up her purse and her briefcase, and left the building. Besides her own car in the parking lot, only the custodian's remained. On her way to her car, she glanced to the school's nearly deserted playground, where, in spite of the slight drizzle, three small boys played.

Ordinarily, she wouldn't have lingered, but Melissa recognized one of the children as Bradley McMillian, so she stood and watched from a distance, her keys still in her hand. Before the change in his family situation, he socialized well and was generally a happy child, and it warmed her heart to see him ignoring the inclement weather to play and laugh with his friends.

As the children frolicked on the playscape, a large dog loped through the opening in the school yard fence and ran toward the boys. The other two children remained on the top of the structure, but Bradley jumped to the ground and ran to the dog.

Instead of wagging its tail, the dog stiffened, flattened its ears back, and lowered its head when Bradley approached it. Because of the dog's odd behavior, Melissa inhaled deeply, about to call out to Bradley not to touch the dog, but before she could get a word out, the dog jumped on top of Bradley, knocking the small child to the ground. Bradley's terrified scream pierced the air.

Melissa's heart stopped, then started up in double-time. She flung her briefcase and keys to the ground and ran with all the speed she could muster toward Bradley and the dog. Frightened cries from the other two children and the angry snarling of the dog magnified the horror of what was happening in front of her.

"Go away! No!" she screamed as she ran, hoping that her presence would scare the dog away.

The dog ignored her completely as it continued to attack little Bradley. He covered his face with his arms, sobbing and screeching in terror. Blood gushed from wounds on his arms, and he kicked his legs, but the dog continued to bite him.

The second she reached them, Melissa grabbed for the dog's collar, but it had none. Failing something solid to hold onto, she frantically tried to grab a handful of the dog's hair to pull it off of Bradley, but the fur was too short and too oily for her to get a grip sufficient to pull the frenzied dog away.

She gritted her teeth, wrapped her hands around its thick neck, and grabbed two handfuls of loose skin, but when she pulled, the combination of the weight of the dog, its oily coat, and the frenzied movement made it impossible to pull the dog away. She continued to scream, but she couldn't distract the dog from its savage attack.

Melissa grabbed her purse, which was still slung over her shoulder, and started whacking the dog, hoping it was heavy enough to either distract it or goad it into defending itself and abandon its attack on Bradley long enough for him to get up and run away.

"Get the custodian!" she called out to the other children as she continued to rain as many blows as possible on the dog's head.

The two children didn't move but cried louder from atop the playscape.

After one well-aimed strike, the dog backed away from Bradley, then crouched in front of her, its ears back and fangs bared.

Her heart raced, both from her frantic run and from fear. She couldn't remember what to do. She knew that when faced with a wild bear, a person was to make eye contact and wild movements, and then run. With a cougar, a person was to back away slowly and not to make eye contact as the cougar considered this an act of aggression.

She didn't know what to do with a mad dog. She only knew that dogs would chase and that she was not to run.

The dog lunged. Automatically, Melissa raised her arms to protect her face. She gritted her teeth and saw stars when it latched onto her arm. The momentum and weight of it knocked her to the ground with a heavy thud and enough force to knock the wind out of her for a few seconds.

As soon as she got her air back, Melissa screamed as loudly as she could while kicking the dog from her position lying on her back. Somehow, she had maintained her grip on her purse when the dog clamped onto her other arm, so she started swinging it wildly, hoping to make contact where it would count.

The dog yelped and released her when her purse made contact with its face. She hit it again and continued to scream. Suddenly, it backed up and ran.

She did her best to quell her own panic and ignore the pain in her arm. She scrambled to her feet and hurried toward Bradley, who was sitting on the ground, his back pressed to one of the support poles for the playscape, where he had been watching the dog since it released him and attacked her.

Melissa crouched in front of him and tried to make her voice sound calm, even though she was screaming inside. "It's gone, Bradley. Can you stand up for me?"

Bradley jumped to his feet, threw his arms tightly around her, and cried so violently she could feel the spasms in his body as he gasped for air. She could tell he was trying to say something, but she couldn't understand a word. The other two children jumped from the playscape and ran home crying, leaving her alone with the hysterical Bradley in the deserted school ground, in the rain.

"Bradley, please let go so I can see you."

She touched his shoulders, squeezed them so he could feel her firm touch, and made him back away. Still holding one of his shoulders, she used her free hand to still first one arm, then the other. The sleeves of his light jacket were ripped to shreds. Bleeding and jagged cuts and puncture wounds all along his tiny forearms nearly caused her to throw up, but she forced herself to remain in control. Bradley needed medical attention, and he needed it fast.

She glanced quickly toward the looming school building. The school nurse had already gone home. She thought about dialing 9-1-1 from the cell phone in her purse, but at this point she couldn't remember if she'd charged the battery, nor did she know if it was in one piece after bashing the dog with it. She didn't have time to waste if it didn't work. Her next option was to force a sobbing injured child to run with her into the building if the custodian hadn't already locked the main door, so she could call an ambulance from the principal's office. It would be quicker to run and make the call without Bradley beside her, but she couldn't make him wait outside while she ran inside alone.

Once more, she looked at her car. The hospital was only a five-minute drive from the school. Whether she called with her cell phone from the parking lot, or if she made it inside the school without having to wait for the custodian, it would be longer to wait for an ambulance than to simply take him herself.

She removed her jacket and wrapped it around Bradley, then escorted him as quickly as he could go without running to her car, and headed for the hospital. The entire time, in order to distract him, she talked about mundane school topics and the upcoming science fair. As she talked, Bradley changed from making the understandable cries of fear to the irregular and more worrisome cries of pain and shock.

It was the longest five minutes of Melissa's life.

Upon arrival at the hospital, the admitting staff ushered them immediately out of the waiting room and into the emergency ward. His crying increased in pitch when she tried to go back to the admitting desk, so they instructed her to fill out the forms later, after Bradley had calmed down, and she could leave him in the care of a doctor or nurse for a few minutes.

They sat together on the bed, with Bradley clutching her tightly. The only time he would release her was when a nurse wrapped gauze around both Bradley's arms and her left arm as they waited for their turn to see an emergency doctor, since Bradley's injuries were not life threatening.

The hospital staff bustled around them, but Melissa felt cut off from the world. The general duty of filling out the forms would have allowed her a distraction to separate herself from the trauma and panic, but she couldn't leave Bradley. Also, now that the situation was somewhat under control, the throbbing of her left arm was becoming more pronounced, making sitting still and trying to keep Bradley calm more difficult.

More than anything, she had to contact Bradley's family. However, away from the records of the school, she didn't have access to emergency phone numbers.

Since she couldn't leave him alone in the ward, Melissa pulled her cell phone out of her purse, deciding now was a good time to see if it still worked. "Bradley, I want to phone home for you. What's your phone number?"

A nurse whose name badge read "Shirley" appeared in front of her. "I'm sorry—you can't use your cell phone in the hospital, Ma'am."

"Sorry. I forgot. I have to call his family."

"There's a phone in the waiting area."

As she looked through the doorway, Bradley's grip around her waist tightened, and his crying worsened, answering her unspoken question of leaving him, even for a couple of minutes. "I think I'll have to wait," she said to the nurse, "but his family will be worried about him. Can you phone for me?"

The nurse pulled out a pencil and paper, and smiled. "I can do that. What's the name and number?"

Melissa gently rubbed Bradley's back. "Nurse Shirley is going to phone your uncle, Bradley. What's his phone number?"

Bradley sniffled, and his words came through gulps for air. "Uncle Josh is at work. I don't know his phone number. I'm supposed to be at Darlene's."

Melissa tried to smile nicely. This was a complication she had not considered. "Then let's give Nurse Shirley Darlene's number."

"I don't know her number."

"Is there anyone at home, Bradley? Your older brother?"

He sniffled again. "Tyler might be home. My number is 555-2318."

Nurse Shirley smiled at Bradley while she spoke to Melissa. "I think I have all the information I need. I'll be right back."

Rather than let Bradley dwell on everything that happened, Melissa thought it best to keep him occupied on other things.

As much as she was curious about his family situation, she spoke only about enjoyable school activities and topics. The entire time she talked with Bradley, which was a very one-sided conversation, she grew increasingly impatient waiting for the nurse to return with word from Bradley's uncle.

Ten minutes later, the nurse finally returned. "I did manage to contact his brother, who is only fifteen." Nurse Shirley trailed her index finger down the paper. "He tried to phone the sitter, but there was no answer. He also tried to contact their uncle at work, but he wasn't there, either, so he left a message. He gave us their pediatrician's number who has confirmed no drug allergies." She paused and handed Melissa a clipboard and pen. "Standard procedure is that as a school staff member you may authorize Bradley's medical treatment based on the medical emergency consent form on file at the school. We've done everything we can to reach his uncle, so now we'll have to wait until someone contacts us. The doctor is ready to see you."

Melissa signed the form and handed it back to the nurse just as a young doctor with stylish wire-framed glasses and carrying a clipboard approached the bed. He pulled the curtain shut around them for some privacy as he examined Bradley's wounds and gave him a mild sedative. Then, between the nurse and Melissa holding Bradley as best they could, the doctor cleaned the wounds, gave him a few stitches, and bandaged him up.

Following that, he did the same to Melissa, making the situation worse because now she didn't know how she was going to drive home with the drugs in her system.

As soon as the last of the tape was applied to the bandaging around her arm, Bradley squirmed his way into her lap.

The doctor stood with his pen poised above the form on the clipboard. "Have either you or the boy had a tetanus shot within the last ten years?"

Melissa shook her head. "I haven't, but I don't know about Bradley."

"Do you know if the dog was up-to-date on its rabies and distemper vaccinations?"

"I don't know. I've never seen the dog before. It just showed up in the school yard."

"Is there any way of locating the dog in the next day or two? I'd rather not assign the rabies treatment for both of you unless it's absolutely necessary." His unspoken message and knotted brows as he glanced at Bradley said all she needed to know about the treatment. She understood the treatment consisted of a painful series of shots, used only as a last resort.

She opened her mouth to ask about a reasonable safety margin when a young man about her age dressed in greasy coveralls and filthy, beat-up work boots burst through the curtain.

two

"Bradley!"

Josh's gut clenched at the sight of poor little Bradley's tear-stained face and bandaged arms. The antiseptic smell of the hospital further turned his stomach.

"Uncle Josh!" Bradley wailed, then launched himself out of a woman's lap and into his chest. The boy threw his arms around Josh's neck and began to sob.

As Josh hugged Bradley tight, he glanced between the woman sitting on the hospital cot and the man in the white lab coat standing beside him. "How is he? What happened?"

He listened to the doctor's brief explanation of the extent of Bradley's wounds and the number of stitches required, followed by an even briefer statement from the woman of how Bradley was attacked by a large stray dog.

Josh held poor Bradley tighter and pressed Bradley's head closer to his chest as the crying subsided to a ragged hiccuping. He couldn't imagine the terror the poor kid had been through; it would have been scary enough for an adult. And if the attack itself wasn't bad enough, he continued to listen as the doctor explained that unless they found the dog and were able to confirm that its vaccinations were up-to-date, especially considering the unprovoked nature of the attack, Bradley would have to go through a painful series of rabies treatments.

The doctor went on to inform Josh that the pediatrician's office had confirmed Bradley didn't need a tetanus shot because he was up-to-date on all his childhood inoculations, and that Bradley would be fine as long as he was kept quiet and the wound kept clean. He told Josh to take Bradley to his own pediatrician in a week to get the stitches removed and for a final checkup.

Numbly, Josh nodded. Taking care of the boys had been a novelty at first, and over the past month they'd developed a routine of what he could only call organized confusion. Most days it was all he could do to make it from one day to the next, but this was unlike anything he could have imagined.

When the doctor left the bedside to tend to another patient, the nurse directed him to the counter where he could sign the necessary forms and pay the bill, which allowed Josh to concentrate more on the woman who was with them.

"I guess you've figured out that I'm Josh McMillian, Bradley's uncle. I want to thank you for taking care of Bradley. You said you're his teacher, but I'm afraid I can't remember your name."

She smiled hesitantly. "It's Melissa Klassen."

Josh forced himself to smile. He didn't know if it was appropriate to shake her hand at a time like this, but thankfully he didn't have the option to do so with Bradley still clinging to him. As grateful as he was for her help and intervention, he didn't want to shake her hand because then she would be able to feel him still trembling.

When he called Tyler back, he'd been expecting to hear that they were again out of some food item. His only thought as he dialed home was annoyance that he would have to stop in at the store on his way home. Instead, Tyler's voice had been filled with panic, and he'd barely been able to understand the jumbled account of Bradley being at the hospital after being attacked by a wild animal. The entire trip to the hospital Josh had pictured the scene of little Bradley struggling with a starving cougar or a crazed raccoon. Relief washed through him to know it was just a dog, in comparison to what it might have been, but with the possibility of rabies not ruled out, the situation remained grave.

One thing for sure, he had not considered anything like this when he agreed to look after his nephews. Even after the worst of the situation was over, his stomach was still upset and his nerves unsteady. If this was how he felt when it was only his nephew, Josh wondered what it was like when something bad happened to one's own child. He wasn't sure he ever wanted to know.

He turned to Bradley's teacher. Although he'd been to both schools to fill out a stack of forms when the guardianship took effect, he hadn't yet had the opportunity to meet any of the kids' teachers.

"I don't know what to say. A simple thank-you doesn't seem like enough. Please let me at least pay for the medical bill for your treatment. I'm really sorry that you were hurt too."

She shook her head, then smiled at him. "Don't worry about it. Since this involved a student and it happened on school grounds, the school will pay for it."

Josh forced himself to smile. No matter who paid, he knew there would never be a way to pay her back sufficiently for what she'd done. Without anyone having said so in front of Bradley, he knew it was by the grace of God that the dog had only bitten Bradley's arms, that it hadn't mauled Bradley's face, as often happened. He'd read in the papers about the horrible things that happened to a child in an unprovoked dog attack. The first thing Josh planned to do when he finally managed to get some quiet time at home was to fall onto his knees and praise God for sparing Bradley from a situation that could have been much worse.

With Bradley still clinging to him, Josh did his best to sign the forms with one hand. Then, rather than writing a check, he handed over his credit card without looking at the total bill. He didn't want to know the amount quite yet. The day had been enough of a shock without that.

During the entire process, he could feel Bradley growing more and more limp in his arms, for which Josh was grateful. With the added incentive of whatever sedative they'd given Bradley going into full effect, Josh knew it would be good for Bradley to sleep off as much as he could, before the full effects of what happened hit him.

Knowing that Bradley had been given a sedative made Josh

wonder if Melissa had also been given something. He figured she would at least have been given a painkiller and some kind of local anesthetic for the stitches.

He stepped closer while she filled out her own release forms. "I just thought of something. You obviously drove here, but are you okay to drive home? Do you need a ride or something?"

The pen froze midword, and she turned her head to look up at him. "You're right. They did tell me not to drive after taking that stuff they gave me. I guess I haven't had time to really think about it, but I would have remembered as soon as I walked out the door. I suppose I do need a ride, but what am I going to do about my car? I don't know how long they'd let me keep it here before I get a parking ticket." She turned her other wrist to check the time, leaving the section of the form unfinished. "You don't think they'd tow it away, do you?"

"Tell you what. I'll drive you home with your car. Then I'll take a cab back here and pick up my van." Inwardly, he cringed at his own suggestion. He hoped she lived fairly close, because the costs for this day, which also included missing time from his job, were continuing to add up quickly. With any luck, she lived on a major bus route that would make it easier and cheaper than a cab to get back to the hospital before too much time had expired. Of course, that meant putting more money in the meter so his van wouldn't get towed away.

She continued writing when the admitting clerk narrowed her eyes and glared at a clock on the wall. "That sounds like a good idea. Actually, I don't live far from here. And don't worry about a cab. By now my neighbors will be home. I'd bet that Dave from next door will be able to drive you back." She paused from writing for long enough to grin upward at him again, doing something strange to Josh's already upset stomach. "He owes me loads of favors and is always asking to return them. This will be something he can do for me."

Josh glanced up at the clock. Normally he wouldn't have accepted such an outlandish offer, but he had so much to do this evening, he couldn't afford to lose more time. "That would be great. But only if it's no trouble for him. Or you. We've already been more than enough trouble for you today."

She smiled up at him. "Don't worry about it. I think we're free to go now."

Except for Melissa giving him directions, silence reigned for most of the drive to her home, confirming his suspicions that she was feeling sleepy from the medication, right along with Bradley. As soon as they arrived at her duplex and settled Bradley onto the couch, she phoned her neighbor, who was more than happy to give Josh a ride back to the hospital to retrieve his van.

When he made it back to her home to pick up Bradley, the two of them were sitting on the couch watching cartoons and eating milk and cookies. Today he didn't care that Bradley wouldn't eat his supper. Seeing Bradley enjoying himself after experiencing such trauma, he almost wanted to join them, except he couldn't because the rest of the family anxiously awaited their arrival back at their own home.

"Come on, Sport. Time to go. Did you say thank you to Miss Klassen for the cookies?"

"Thank you, Miss Klassen!" Bradley smiled and wrapped his little arms around her, but winced when he started to squeeze, indicating that the medication was starting to wear off.

Josh stepped closer to pick Bradley up. "Yes, thank you, Miss Klassen. I don't know what we would have done without you. If there's anything I can ever do for you, please let me know."

She smiled politely, then struggled with a bad attempt to stifle a yawn. "I'll do that. Good night, Mr. McMillian."

Bradley shook his head so fast Josh could feel his whole body shake in his arms. "No! My dad is gone away with my mom until she gets better. That's Uncle Josh! Remember?"

One corner of her mouth quirked up. "Then good night, Uncle Josh."

Josh nodded. "Good night, Miss Klassen."

He quickly settled Bradley into his booster seat and headed for home.

"Miss Klassen is sure nice, isn't she, Uncle Josh?"

"Yes, she's very nice."

"And brave."

"Yes, and brave."

"And strong."

Josh smiled. Developing a bad case of hero worship was a much better alternative than lingering over the horror of the whole experience. "Yes, she's very strong. I'll bet she's smart, too."

He glanced in the rearview mirror to view Bradley's place in the center of the van, since it wasn't safe to put a child his size in the front seat because of the air bag. Bradley was nodding so fast his hair bounced. Josh returned his attention to the road.

"Yes, she's super smart. And she's really pretty too."

Josh smiled back at Bradley's enthusiasm. Admittedly, he hadn't seen his teacher at her best, but still, if he had to be honest, he'd seen better-looking women. Not that there was anything wrong with her, but he didn't usually go for the blond, blue-eyed types. All in all, she was fairly ordinary— average height, nothing striking about her, especially her hair, which was shoulder length and a bit on the straggly side. Not anywhere close to fashionably thin, she was still by no means fat. Although he couldn't see anything particularly spectacular about her, because of how she'd saved Bradley from things he didn't want to think about Josh could see her strength and beauty lay where it counted most, and that was deep inside.

Josh suspected that inner beauty was what Bradley saw through the eyes of a child, because children interpreted things at a more basic level than adults.

"Okay, we're home now. I can see the blinds moving. Everyone is really anxious to see you."

As soon as he opened the door of the van to get out, the front door of the house opened. Without thinking about what was happening behind him, he ignored the rush of bodies noisily scrambling down the sidewalk and opened the sliding side door to undo Bradley's seat belt. Behind him, he heard a sudden silence as the rest of his nephews jostled for position, waiting for him to step aside so they could see what happened to their brother. Just as Bradley stepped into the opening ready to hop out of the van and to the ground, a bark sounded behind him.

He gritted his teeth. The last one out of the house had forgotten to close the front door, and the dog got out.

Josh turned around. "Cleo! No!" he shouted as he scrambled to block the dog. As a yellow Labrador, Cleo was heavy and hard to stop once she made her mind up to do something, especially once she had gained the advantage of momentum.

He made a grab for Cleo as she bounded past him, but missed. Cleo jumped onto Bradley the second the boy's feet touched the ground, her large paws landing squarely on Bradley's chest. His heart pounded at Bradley's squeal when Bradley fell to the ground with Cleo on top of him.

Josh thought he might throw up. He barely made one step toward them when the squealing turned to giggles as Cleo licked Bradley in the face, stopping Josh dead in his tracks.

That Bradley wasn't going to be afraid of dogs gave something else for Josh to be thankful for in his prayers tonight.

He swiped his hand through his hair, exhaling in a rush. "Come on, guys. Let's get into the house. It's way past supper time. Who wants spaghetti? If we hurry, Kyle can still make it to swimming lessons, but I think Bradley is going to miss Cubs today. And who's got homework? Andrew, don't you have a test tomorrow?"

The combined moan wasn't unexpected. "Uncle Josh!"

❧

The phone rang just as Melissa stuck her toothbrush in her mouth. She ran to catch the phone, wondering who could possibly be calling at this time of day. She had to be out the door in five minutes in order to arrive at the school early to talk to the principal about the incident with Bradley McMillian.

"Hello?" she mumbled around her toothbrush.

"Miss Klassen?"

Melissa removed the toothbrush from her mouth and smiled. Usually it was only children who addressed her so, but this was a deep, flowing baritone voice. She recognized the caller before he identified himself. "Hello, Uncle Josh."

She heard him clearing his throat. "I thought I'd call and make sure you were okay."

"Yes, I'm fine. Thank you for asking." She smiled, hearing little Bradley's voice in the background bombarding his uncle with questions until Josh assured Bradley that all was well and asked the boy to hush.

"Great. Well, I won't keep you. I guess you're probably almost on your way out the door."

"Yes, I am."

"Sorry to bother you. Good-bye, Miss Klassen."

"No problem. Good-bye, Uncle Josh."

With a quick glance at the time, she ran back to the bathroom to finish brushing her teeth, grabbed her travel mug of coffee from the kitchen, and ran to the door.

She managed to arrive at the school early enough to talk to the principal and fill out the necessary reports, including something for the police about the dog, but she didn't have time to complete the medical forms before she had to be inside her classroom with enough time to prepare for the children's entrance for the morning.

To her surprise, Bradley walked in with the rest of the children, proudly showing off his bandages. She hadn't thought he would be attending classes today, but it did her heart good to see the child, who was normally quiet, bravely explaining to all his friends what had happened.

Not long after the bell to start classes sounded, the principal's voice came booming over the intercom advising everyone that a student had been attacked by a stray dog the day before. He then described the dog according to Melissa's report, followed by a warning to the children to beware of that particular stray or any dog and not to approach any animal they didn't know. The principal then requested that if anyone had any information about the dog in question to contact the school office, animal control, or the police department immediately. Melissa knew that a notice would be printed and passed out to the children to take home before the end of the school day.

The morning passed by quickly because of the science fair in the gymnasium, although the tension was high as the students eagerly anticipated the results of the vote for best in the class. Following the first vote, announcements would be made of the winner in each grade, then in each division. In the evening, after the parents had been given the opportunity to browse through all the exhibits, they would announce the school winner, who would go to the district's competition.

Melissa didn't want to tell her students, but she knew none of her grade one class would make it that high. When the results were announced, she had a small "prize" for every student in the class ready and waiting, each one named as best in something, even if it was only for the best use of colored glue.

When the bell for lunch break sounded, those who were staying inside the building hurried to get their backpacks and hustled back to their desks.

"Miss Klassen?"

Melissa turned to see Bradley's hand waving back and forth in the air. "Yes?"

"My juice spilled all over my lunch, and it messed up my backpack. Can I phone Uncle Josh to bring me a new lunch?"

"I thought your uncle was at work?"

Bradley reached inside the neckline of his bright red T-shirt and pulled out a thin chain with what looked like a dog tag hanging on it. "Uncle Josh wrote down his work number and also Darlene's. That's my sitter. So I can call him anytime I need him."

Melissa tried not to smile in front of him as she admired Uncle Josh's unique idea.

"Yes, you may call him, but if he doesn't have time to come all this way, I'll share my lunch with you."

Bradley dashed from the room before Melissa finished her sentence and returned within three minutes. He dumped his entire lunch in the garbage pail except for his empty thermos, then sat at his desk. "Uncle Josh is coming," he said with a big smile that extended nearly ear to ear. "My Uncle Josh is really nice. Do you think Uncle Josh is nice?"

"Yes, your uncle is very nice."

"Uncle Josh makes good spaghetti. He even made pizza once."

"Uncle Josh sounds like a good cook."

"Yes, he is. He's good at fixing cars, too." Bradley's smile widened as he sat at his desk, not moving a muscle. He folded his hands on the desk in front of him, straightened his back, and planted his feet firmly on the floor while he waited very patiently, especially for a six year old.

Melissa checked her watch a number of times as everyone else in the room ate their lunches while Bradley continued to sit as still as a statue. Melissa wondered how she could get the entire class to sit like that at the same time, even for a few minutes.

When only five minutes remained of the children's lunch break, Bradley's uncle strode into the classroom carrying a brown paper bag displaying the logo of a local fast-food restaurant. Melissa noticed he wore exactly the same type of clothing as the day before, coveralls streaked with oil and grime and the well-used work boots. This time, though, his hair was even messier.

Bradley sprang to his feet. "Uncle Josh!"

"Here's something for lunch, Bradley. I don't know how your juice spilled. I thought I tightened it this morning. Sorry about that."

Bradley hurriedly emptied a cheeseburger and fries out of the bag while his uncle handed him a soft drink. "That's okay, Uncle Josh. Do you want to talk to Miss Klassen?"

Melissa crossed her arms, sat on the edge of her desk, and watched the two of them in action. The love Bradley held for his uncle shone through both in his eyes and in his smile. She didn't need to talk to his uncle. While she could question the nutritional quality of the lunch, Josh was doing his best as a substitute parent when he dropped everything and hurried to the school with an emergency replacement meal.

"Maybe another time. I have to hurry and get back to work. See you at supper time, Sport."

Melissa stood and looked up at the clock. "Thanks for coming, Uncle Josh. I hope you're not late getting back to work."

He grinned, and the start of very attractive laugh lines appeared briefly at the corners of his eyes, probably amused that a woman her age would keep calling him "uncle."

"Actually, I'm working right now. I'm taking a car for a test run before I give it back to the owner with a clean bill of health."

She'd never considered that a car could be sick but chose to say nothing rather than keep him with aimless chitchat.

Melissa watched the flash of his blue coveralls disappear around the corner out the classroom door. Just as Bradley had said, Josh did seem like a nice man. She had to admire the spirit and fortitude of anyone who would take on five boys who were not his own, jumping in with both feet to become an instant single parent. That he was handling them right was proven by Bradley's obvious love and admiration. He seemed to be living up to the responsibility and challenge of balancing a job and five active boys, although she knew he would continue to have struggles, as every parent did.

She sighed while placing the empty containers of her own lunch into her drawer, regretting that she couldn't have met him another way. Even though it was not stated in her contract, there was very much an unspoken rule at the school that the teachers were not to have a relationship with any of the single parents of their students unless they already knew them from outside the school, and even then it was discouraged.

While the school could never enforce such a rule on paper, it had been made very clear when she was hired.

The ruling stemmed from an incident years ago when one of the other teachers had been dating a student's father, supposedly a single parent who wasn't single at all. The following scandal affected not only those directly involved, but a major percentage of the school population and, most notably, that teacher's own class where most of the students ended up hating the teacher involved. It eroded the reputation of the teacher and nearly destroyed her career, because even though she had been a victim, gossip and innuendo followed her even after she had to change schools.

Melissa definitely respected the wisdom of that decision. True, it was a worst-case scenario, but she could also imagine what might happen to the general morale and atmosphere inside the classroom if a teacher dated any student's parent, even someone really single. Favoritism, real or imagined, would definitely be a major issue. Also, in most cases the relationship would not see through to marriage, and strained or hurt feelings would follow the breakup, as well as for a considerable time afterward. No teacher could perform adequately under those conditions.

After Bradley wolfed down the last of his fries, Melissa sent the children out into the playground and spent the rest of her lunch break in the staff room. While she filled her coffee mug, she listened to a couple of the other teachers discussing two of Bradley's brothers, Ryan and Kyle, who also attended that school. All three boys had needed to make major adjustments in their lives, and it appeared they were slowly working through the process of the separation from their parents, as well as getting used to the shift in authority with their young uncle moving into their home and taking charge.

No matter how well they were doing on the surface, Melissa knew right then there was something that she personally could do. Not only did she need to pray for little Bradley this weekend but also for his whole family.

three

"Get dressed? Why?"

Josh stood in the middle of the living room as he fastened the cuffs on his shirt. It felt good to wear something that required buttons again, unlike the usual T-shirt and jeans he wore under his coveralls at work every day or around the house in the evenings. He also liked the feeling of wearing good leather shoes instead of his heavy steel-toed safety work boots all day.

He straightened the knot on his tie. "We're going to church. And don't pick anything with holes in the knees."

"Church!" a chorus of voices bellowed around him.

"That's right. I haven't been to church since I moved in with you guys, and it's about time. Instead of going back to my old neighborhood, I've picked a nice church close by that I think will have lots of kids everyone's age, probably even some of the kids you go to school with every day. So, everybody, get moving. We're going to all be in the van in precisely thirty minutes."

"But I'm not finished with the level!"

"Too bad, Ryan. Save the game, turn it off, and get dressed. I hope you've already had your cereal." He didn't bother to ask if they had brushed their teeth because the ensuing scramble answered his question, just like most mornings. Even though Josh could never understand how they did it, everyone was in the van at exactly the right time, although he noticed Andrew's laces weren't tied.

"Why do we hafta go to church? Mom and Dad never made us go to church."

"What's the matter, Tyler? Don't you believe in God?"

"Yeah, I believe in God. So what?"

"So that's why you go to church."

"What if church is boring?"

A round of "yeahs" echoed around him as he turned the key to start the engine.

"Then it's up to you to make it unboring. All you have to do is pay attention and think about what's being said."

"Why do you go to church, Uncle Josh?"

He turned to smile briefly at Tyler as he backed onto the street. "To worship God and be with other people who believe in God like I do. And then I get to listen to the pastor tell me stuff about God, so I can learn something."

A rare silence filled the van, but it didn't last long.

"Learn something? You mean church is like school?"

"Well, no. Just see for yourselves, okay?"

Not much was said on the journey until they pulled into the large parking lot, where Josh heard mumbles of wonderment that there were so many people there. He smiled to himself when he heard Ryan comment softly that maybe church wasn't going to be so bad, after all.

Fortunately the kids were quiet and stuck close to him while he checked the place out. From the crowd already assembled and the size of the sanctuary, he judged the congregation to be about a thousand people, which was more than he was used to but was probably best for the kids to integrate themselves.

He didn't know if the kids were supposed to go directly into the Sunday school classrooms or sit with the rest of the congregation until dismissed, so he took the lead from watching other families who were seated in the sanctuary, kids and all, waiting for the service to begin.

When more people started filing into the sanctuary as the time neared ten o'clock, Josh pointed his nephews toward the sanctuary opening. They hadn't gone more than a few steps when he heard a familiar female voice behind him.

"Uncle Josh? Bradley?"

At the sound of his name, Bradley immediately stopped walking, causing Ryan to bump into him, then Andrew tripped over Ryan, who barely managed to right himself before Andrew hit the floor.

Josh squeezed his eyes shut for a second before he forced himself to smile and reclaim his dignity as he turned around. "Hi, Miss Klassen. This is a pleasant surprise to see you in church. I don't think you have to call me 'Uncle Josh' here." He covered his heart with his open hand. "I'm not in school today."

Her cheeks turned a cute shade of pink, which Josh thought quite appealing.

"I guess you can call me Melissa today then, Unc. . .uh. . . Josh." Her cheeks darkened even more, and Josh had to try very hard not to laugh.

He glanced around them, but everyone in the area appeared to be going about their own business. No one lingered waiting for a lull in their conversation.

"Are you alone today? Would you like to sit with us? I'd appreciate it if you could let me know a little about the routine here. I see some of the kids' friends, and I'm hoping we can plug in here, since it's so close to home."

She smiled at him. Suddenly Josh thought she looked much prettier than in the classroom on Friday afternoon, but he couldn't figure out why; after all, she wore the same kind of clothes.

"Yes, certainly. I've been coming here for years, so I'm fairly sure I can answer most of your questions. But I think that's going to have to wait until after. We really should get a seat."

He nodded. "Of course."

It pleased Josh to discover that he knew most of the songs this congregation sang during the worship time, although he was somewhat distracted watching the five boys. Before he took his place as their legal guardian, he had rarely missed a Sunday service, attending either alone or with friends, most of whom were single adults like him. For the moment the boys appeared to be enjoying the music, although Josh knew it wouldn't last because they weren't used to sitting still for prolonged periods of time.

As he expected, when they were asked to stand, Ryan and Andrew began elbowing each other in the ribs and giggling, disturbing not only himself but also those around them. He hunkered down into a rather undignified squat and settled them down as best he could, then tried to return his thoughts to the words of the song, once he found out where they were and how much he'd missed.

In the past, he'd frequently become annoyed when parents couldn't control their children during the service, but he had a bad feeling that he was going to learn the hard way it wasn't as easy as it looked. He recalled a few families from his home church whose children always sat nearly still and actively participated in the worship time. He suddenly developed a healthy dose of respect for them.

When the worship leader dismissed the children for Sunday school, Melissa rose as well.

He looked up and touched her arm to get her attention. "Where are you going?"

She leaned down to whisper her reply. "I'm teaching this week. In fact, I'll be Bradley's Sunday school teacher today and for the next month. Your timing to pick this as your first Sunday here is good. Bradley will feel more comfortable in a strange place since he knows me, as well as a couple of other children from his grade. There is Sunday school for up to grade seven, so you'll have only the older children with you for the sermon. I have to go now. See you later, Josh."

Before he knew it, all the younger kids from the congregation, Melissa, and a number of other adults were gone, leaving a strange hush in the large room after the rustle of clothing and thudding of running feet echoed out the exit door and down the hall.

The pastor was a gifted speaker, evidenced not only because Josh found himself enjoying the message, but because Andrew and Tyler were also paying attention most of the time. He found Tyler often sneaking peeks across the room to where a number of teenagers sat in the back corner, which reminded him to ask Melissa about the youth group. He had a feeling that if he encouraged Tyler to take his friend Allyson, it would be good for everyone.

After the service closed, Josh made the rounds with Andrew and Tyler in tow to pick up the other three from their Sunday school rooms in the basement.

Josh left Bradley until last.

While the boys either checked out the room and its contents or stood around in the hall talking with friends from school who also attended, Josh approached Melissa. He picked up the eraser and helped erase the lesson notes and pictures from the whiteboard while she gathered the papers and felt pens.

He checked over his shoulder to make sure he wasn't in hearing range of any of his nephews, then stepped closer to Melissa when she made her way to the desk at the front of the row. "So how did Bradley do?"

She lowered the stack of notebooks to the counter. "Well. . . ," she drawled, not looking at him. "He was well behaved and fit in nicely with the rest of the class."

"I suppose that's good. But what I meant was, how did he do with the class and lesson in general? He's never been to church in his life, so this was really different for him."

Melissa raised her head. "That explains a lot, actually. He really didn't know anything, not even the major names in the Bible." She paused to smile. "Except Jesus. He knew that. Also, he was a little disruptive while we were praying, and when we passed the tin for the offering, he wanted to take money out, not put it in."

Josh felt his cheeks heat up. "Oops. I forgot to give them some change before they went off to their classes. You see, Brian and Sasha never took the kids to church. They've never had any spiritual nurturing or any experience praying, not even saying grace at the table. Brian and Sasha never even paused for a word of prayer on Christmas Day. And now that I think about it, they didn't on Thanksgiving Day, either. That's something I plan to start, but I couldn't start them praying without giving them a basic understanding of who God is and what prayer is all about. I've had them over a month now, and I figured this would be a good time to start. There's been a lot of things to get used to before I made this kind of change in their lives."

He grinned and straightened his tie. "It's taken awhile, but we're getting used to living together, although I think it's a bigger adjustment for me than it is for them. They've always been together as a large group, but up until recently, it's just been me and Cleo."

Her brows knotted. "Cleo?"

"Yes. She's made the adjustment to living with the boys much more easily than I did. I was worried about it for awhile, but all the boys just love her, and she loves them all just the same."

She opened her mouth to speak, but Ryan came bursting into the room, halting their conversation.

"Uncle Josh! Uncle Josh! Did you know that Sarah comes here too!"

He bent down to address Ryan. "That's great. Anyone else you know?"

Bradley and Kyle chose that moment to come in, running. "Uncle Josh! Uncle Josh! I saw Brandon!"

"And I saw Cody!"

Josh gave up any attempt at conversations with any of them. He stood and turned to Melissa. "I guess I should go find Andrew and Tyler. I was thinking of making their first day of church attendance a memorable experience and taking them out for lunch, if the restaurant can handle us. Would you care to join us? No promises on being quiet or civilized, though."

"Well, I. . . ," her voice trailed off as Bradley began tugging on the hem of her skirt.

"Please, Miss Klassen? We'll behave. And I promise we won't throw anything."

Josh felt his cheeks heat up again. He rested his palm on top of Bradley's head. "I don't think that came out right. They really don't throw things in public restaurants. It's kind of a private joke. You know. Kids." He tried to laugh, but it fell flat.

"I guess I could. You said you had a few questions about the church. I can give you a rundown of the groups and activities they have on a regular basis, if you want."

"Great. I'd like that. We've got one empty seat in the van. Would you like to come with us?"

Andrew and Tyler chose that moment to saunter into the classroom, which was now empty except for Melissa and his family, which, come to think of it, totaled seven people, making it not so empty after all.

"I think I'll take my own car and meet you there. Where are we going?"

⋙

Melissa followed the McMillian family van into the parking lot of a respectable midpriced restaurant that served hamburger platters as their mainstay menu item.

She found a parking spot and had just turned off the engine when she glanced in their direction and began to watch the horde of male bodies exit from the van.

As she watched them pile out, she wondered why Cleo wasn't with them. The more she thought about Cleo, the more it puzzled her. Not that Josh's private life was any of her business—she'd just met him, and her only contact with him was because of his responsibility of guardianship for one of her students. But since the change in Bradley's family situation had affected Bradley's schoolwork, that made it her business, at least on a professional level.

She'd known Josh was single according to the form she'd seen at the school regarding the change in the legal guardianship, but apparently he wasn't as single as she'd first assumed. She'd never heard Bradley mention his aunt Cleo, but if Josh and Cleo weren't married, Cleo wouldn't be an aunt, simply his uncle's girlfriend. Perhaps just being his uncle's girlfriend wasn't worthy of a mention in the eyes of a small boy.

However, Josh's reference to Cleo made it sound like they were living together, and now living together with Josh's nephews.

Because of Josh's familiarity with the general routine at the church, his knowledge of the worship songs, as well as his desire to share the gospel and the message of the love of Jesus with his nephews, she could tell he was not a new Christian. Being an established Christian, he also would know better than to live with a woman without the benefit of marriage. While she knew that the parents of some of her students over the years were living together and having children without being married, as a Christian Josh knew such a lifestyle was wrong in the eyes of God.

Melissa wondered if this was the reason he left his previous church—which was where he should have taken the boys—where he should have had friends who could help him teach the boys about the love of God in their lives, not to someplace new to all of them.

Maybe he had been reprimanded because he was living with Cleo and chose not to make any changes in his relationship or lifestyle.

The more she thought about it, the less reason she could see for not going back to one's own home church unless there was something preventing him from doing so. She only wished she knew what it was, and if it was because of the situation with Cleo.

She, too, wanted to see the entire family come to know Jesus as their Lord and Savior. Her heart especially went out to Bradley, not only as her student, but because she truly liked the little boy.

Therefore, her first step would be to learn more about the relationship between Josh and Cleo. When she got to know Josh better, then she could gently suggest to him to look at the error of his ways.

In the forefront of her heart was the worry that he would be a better Christian witness to his nephews if he put himself under God's moral laws and practiced what he preached in terms of general obedience to everything God's Word outlined. Pursuing him for such a reason would not only put her in an awkward position on a personal basis with Josh, but she also had her reputation at the school to consider.

She owed Principal Swain no explanation in regards to anything she did in her personal life, which meant both her friendships and her romantic involvements. Yet, very little in the life a teacher could remain private when young children were involved, especially in the close community of the school where word traveled fast. Principal Swain would be very interested when he discovered she was seeing the acting parent of one of her students, especially since Josh was not exactly single in the eyes of the general population. What was wrong in the eyes of God not withstanding, her actions would quickly meet with his disapproval, even though there would be no courtship involved.

Principal Swain's mandate wasn't in their contract, nor could he fire her or take any disciplinary action for anything regarding her personal life. However, he could and would easily magnify any minor problems or disturbances to a point where they would sully her so-far-spotless teaching record. She couldn't afford to have that happen.

Melissa closed her eyes for a second, reminding herself that God's rules were more important than man's rules. Her responsibility as a Christian lay in gently pushing Josh in the path the Lord demanded he should go, and that meant the sanctity of marriage, not common-law.

In order to do that, she would have to develop a friendship with Josh, which could be tricky with Bradley involved. Knowing Bradley as she did, she didn't think he would expect favoritism or special treatment, but a six year old wasn't always predictable. Bradley was a sweet little boy and going through a difficult time in his young life, so she couldn't give him unrealistic expectations of her friendship with his uncle. On the other hand, Bradley needed extra love and attention at this difficult time in his life. Melissa decided she could easily afford to show him a little favoritism, as long as she expected and demanded that his schoolwork meet with the expectations of his level, which at grade one weren't unreasonably high.

Last of all, Melissa had to consider Josh and Cleo. All she needed to do was to gain his respect enough to nudge him in the right direction in the eyes of God without stepping into the middle of an existing relationship, and certainly not to cause division. She prayed she could do that without compromising her own Christian witness.

With her mind made up, the first thing she had to do was to find more information about Cleo.

Melissa locked up her car and joined the McMillians as Bradley hopped onto the pavement and one of the older boys slid the side door shut. "Here I am. I guess we can go in now."

Josh checked the van door to make sure it was locked and dropped the keys into his pocket. "Do you know if this place has lots of large tables? I know that when we're trying to seat so many, we often have to wait a long time."

"I'm not sure. There's only one way to find out."

Once inside, they didn't have to wait too long for a table that would seat seven, especially considering it was Sunday. As the waitresses pushed two tables together for them, a little voice piped up beside her.

"You want to sit beside Uncle Josh, don't you, Miss Klassen?"

She smiled at Bradley. She would have rather sat across from him in order to see him while she talked to him, but she didn't want to make a scene. "Yes, Bradley, I think that would be nice."

When she took the chair beside Josh, Bradley sat on her other side. "I bet Uncle Josh will let you order anything you want, even dessert—right, Uncle Josh?"

Without waiting for Josh to answer, Bradley leaned his head closer to her and lowered his voice to what he probably thought was a discreet whisper, even though Melissa was sure the people at the next table heard him quite plainly. "The kid's meal comes with dessert, but yours doesn't. But you gotta eat your vegabulls, or Uncle Josh won't let you have any dessert, even if it did come with your meal."

"I promise to eat my veg-e-ta-bles, Bradley. But I might not want dessert."

His eyes widened. "Then can I have it?"

Melissa heard Josh's sharp intake of breath on the other side of her. "Bradley! That's enough!"

Melissa turned to Josh, whose cheeks were a charming shade of pink.

She rested her fingertips on his forearm. "It's okay, Uncle Josh. I'm an elementary schoolteacher, and I promise there's very little a child could do or say that would surprise me."

"Well, I don't know. . . . I'm sure these guys can come up with something."

A tugging on her sleeve made Melissa turn back to Bradley.

"If we come to church every Sunday, can you always come out to lunch with us, Miss Klassen?"

"I don't know, Bradley. I may not be invited."

The tugging increased in speed and intensity. "You're invited! And you can even sit with us in church on Sunday! Uncle Josh will let you have dessert, even if you don't eat all your vegabulls. Right, Uncle Josh?"

Josh's voice came out in a lower pitch than she'd heard before. "Please, Bradley, leave Miss Klassen alone. And can't you give one of your brothers a turn to talk?"

The oldest boy plunked his elbows on the table and rested his chin in his palms. "I don't know. He seems to be doing fine for all of us."

Josh choked on his coffee, and a couple of the other boys, whose names Melissa wasn't quite sure she could match to the rightful owners, started to giggle.

Rather than leave poor Josh out to dry, after their orders were taken, Melissa changed the subject to the usual weekly and weekend activities happening around the church, especially noting the Boys Club and the youth group meetings, as well as a quick rundown of some of the adult Bible studies, many of which were planned on the same night as the kids' activities to avoid baby-sitting problems.

When two waitresses arrived with their meals, she found it odd not to stop for a prayer of thanks for the food, especially on a Sunday following a church service, but the younger boys dug into their food before all the plates were distributed. She didn't want to think of what mealtime was like at their home, where there would be less formality than in a restaurant setting.

Josh leaned toward her. "I know what you're thinking. I'll be working on that too."

From the looks of things, Josh had a lot to work on besides getting them to eat all their vegetables. She wasn't absolutely positive if he meant the lack of a prayer before eating or the mayhem in general, although considering the situation he found himself cast in, the boys seemed generally happy, at least on the outside. She knew that often what went on on the inside was another matter.

Despite the general confusion, Melissa had a wonderful time among the active family. Their hijinks and the silly schoolboy jokes amused her, and she knew that if Josh asked her next Sunday to join them, she would again, whether or not Cleo decided to attend with the family.

The trip into the parking lot became another blur of activity. Before she separated herself from the little entourage, Josh stepped aside with her while the boys piled into the van.

"Thanks for coming with us and for sitting with us in church. I want to make regular church attendance a part of their lives, and with that I hope to be able to share the gospel with them in a meaningful way, instead of church just being something they 'do.' "

She smiled. "That's great. And thanks for lunch."

He smiled back. "Since Bradley asked, will we see you next week?"

If he was coming with the boys, then most definitely.

"Probably. See you next Sunday, then. Good-bye, Josh."

four

"Hello? Josh?"

Josh found himself smiling at the sound of the voice on the other end of the phone. Then, he realized that because it was Monday morning and he was taking the call at work, she was at work, too, which meant she was calling from the school—and that meant the call was about Bradley.

His stomach knotted. "Good morning, Melissa. Is something wrong?"

"No, nothing is wrong. I'm phoning to say that the principal got a call from one of the residents in the neighborhood. It's about the dog that bit Bradley and me. They've identified the dog. It was up-to-date on all its shots, so we don't have to worry about rabies or anything."

"That's really good. But what about the dog? Is there a police report to fill out and stuff like that? When something like this happens, doesn't a process start to put the dog down? Or press charges or something?"

"Actually, we don't have to worry about it. The dog got hit by a car over the weekend, so no one has to make a decision on what to do about it. I've got mixed feelings about that myself; it's kind of sad, but it's been taken out of our hands. So I guess that's a good thing."

Josh wiped his greasy hand down the front of his coveralls and stuck it in his pocket. He turned to face the wall as he spoke because he didn't want a customer to listen to him on a personal call. "Yeah, I guess. I've been doing a lot of praying over that. Although it's not exactly the way I hoped it would happen, either. The most important thing is that Bradley is fine and you're fine."

"I know what you mean. I love dogs, and even when it's

not a nice dog, it still upsets me to hear when something like that happens."

"Yeah." Josh knew the first thing he was going to do when he got home was to give Cleo a big hug and an extra dog biscuit. "I have to get back to work—I guess you do too."

"It's recess time, so I'm okay for a few minutes yet, but I guess you're not on a coffee break, are you?"

He heard the customer behind him shuffling in the magazine pile. He hadn't had time to take a break today. He still had a lot of catching up to do from the time he missed on Thursday, which his boss was going to let him make up. "No, I'm not. I'll catch you another time, I guess."

They said their good-byes, and Josh returned his attention to the problem on his customer's car. After the customer left, Josh pulled the car into the bay to begin working on it. As he tinkered, his thoughts returned to Melissa.

Even though they'd been far from alone yesterday, it had been good to be in the company of a single woman for no real purpose except to socialize and relax, if being in charge of five boys could in any way be called relaxing. Melissa had barely blinked when Kyle had accidentally dropped one of his fries into her coffee, and she'd been a tremendous help in making them take turns with the ketchup without fighting. She'd also been the one to catch Ryan loosening the lid to the salt before he passed it to Andrew to shake onto his fries. Even Tyler liked her because she talked to him differently than the younger boys, instead of lumping them all together as he had seen people often do.

Josh smiled. The woman was indeed good with kids.

Josh's smile dropped, and he squeezed his eyes shut for a second before he resumed his work. He'd always thought Theresa was good with kids too. She'd also taught Sunday school in his home church, but she wasn't a teacher by trade like Melissa. They'd even talked about kids from time to time, and at the same time, Theresa had started to hint about wedding bells.

Even though he didn't see fireworks when he was with Theresa, he'd thought she was the right woman for him to spend his life with, until he made the decision to look after his nephews when Brian and Sasha went to Switzerland. Theresa's scathing comments and inability to understand how important this was to him, especially since he and Brian no longer had their parents, had cut him to the core. The spiteful things she'd said leading to their breakup had taught him a few things about her he hadn't seen before, making him grateful to have discovered them before he made a serious commitment.

It also started him thinking about his situation and the projected reality of how long it could last, and where his life could go in the process. Theresa's final barbed words were that Sasha was never going to get better, and no woman in her right mind would ever want to date him, an instant adoptive father of five boys, one of them only ten years younger than himself.

The trouble was, Theresa was probably right on both counts. Looking back, he'd always thought Sasha to be a bit unstable. Only twelve when his brother had married Sasha, at the time he'd thought her a little strange, even though from a child's perspective he couldn't say what it was—he only knew that something wasn't quite right with her. As the years went on, she had become more and more unstable. Both her mental and physical health worsened, and no doctors had been able to help her. Now she had progressed to such a point that Brian thought this clinic in Switzerland was her only hope of a recovery after a lifetime of suffering.

Because of that, his family needed him, and they had to be his first priority. Therefore, he didn't have the time, and certainly not the energy, to both raise the kids and date, especially to find someone who knew him the way Theresa had, before the kids came into his life full time. Those kids needed a lot of love and attention, and he was the only one to give it to them since their parents were gone.

Therefore, Theresa's unkind words about him being single for as long as he had the boys probably would be true. It wasn't like he was a regular single father with one or two young boys. There were five of them, one of them a teenager.

And thus ended his future love life.

Josh turned his concentration to adjusting a timing belt until his stomach grumbled, making him check the clock, which was exactly in sync with his stomach. It was just few minutes after noon, and lunchtime. Josh wiped his hands and had just stuffed the rag into the back pocket of his coveralls when Rick called him to take the phone.

As he hung up, he looked up at the time again, then quickly checked his wallet. "Hey, Rick, I've got to go to the school again, so I'll take my lunch, and I'll add a few more minutes to take that blue Ford for a test drive. I'll be back in three quarters of an hour."

&

"Hello again, Uncle Josh. It's been so long since we spoke."

Josh smiled back at Melissa as he handed Bradley the hamburger, fries, and the drink. "Yeah. I thought I tightened the lid to that thermos better this morning, especially after last Friday. We've got to stop meeting like this."

She smiled back, and Josh's breath caught. He didn't know why he hadn't thought of her as very pretty, because she certainly had a unique warmth and a very pretty smile.

"Josh? Is something wrong? You're looking at me funny."

He narrowed one eye. "Have you done something different with your hair since yesterday?"

"Uh. . .no. . . ," her voice trailed off as she ran her fingers into her hair to fluff it.

"Never mind, it must be the light or something. Actually, this is kind of a good opportunity for me to ask you a question. I've got about ten minutes before I have to head back to work. I wanted to thank you for encouraging the kids yesterday. We talked about the Boys Club and the youth group, and they're all interested in going." He paused to grin. "Even though it's going to mean another night of driving them around, I'm looking forward to it. Now I can go to the adult Bible study on the same night. I've never had to think about it before, but baby-sitting can sure get expensive. I've missed attending weekly Bible studies, so this is a good chance for me to plug in while they're all off doing something else. It's going to be great getting involved in church activities again."

"That's wonderful, Josh. What about Cleo?"

Josh let out a short laugh. "Cleo? She'll just sleep the whole time everybody's gone. She spends a lot of time home alone. Actually, I think she sleeps a lot."

"Does that mean you'd go to the adult evening Bible study alone?"

"Yeah, although it's been a long time since I've been to one by myself. I wouldn't think I'd be the only person going stag, would I?"

The light touch of her fingertips on his arm startled him—first, that she'd actually touched him, but secondly, he hadn't realized they'd been standing so close. Then he realized it had been him who approached her and stood close so Bradley wouldn't hear what they were talking about.

"Our church is quite large, and we have an assistant pastor who is also a counselor. He specializes in couples counseling. Would you like me to get his card for you?"

All he could do was blink in wonderment at her perception of his situation. He had no idea how she'd known that he'd recently split up with someone, and he chided himself for being so transparent. He thought he'd done a good job in overcoming the sting of Theresa leaving him, and it made him wonder if it showed that much. "No, that's okay, but thanks for suggesting it. I've been thinking about it since all this started, and I decided she's not the person I'd marry, anyway."

She withdrew her hand as fast as if she'd been stung.

He checked his watch. "I think I'd better be heading back to work. But first I'm going to say bye to Bradley. Thanks again for the phone call this morning, Melissa. I'm glad both of you are going to be okay."

At his own words, he couldn't help but glance at her arms, which were covered by long sleeves, efficiently hiding the bandages. He'd done the same with Bradley's clothing.

Bradley had just stuffed the last of the fries into his mouth as Josh approached his desk. "Sorry about your lunch, Sport. But I know you like the fries better than the sandwich."

"Yeah, Uncle Josh. Thanks. Did you have a nice talk with Miss Klassen?"

"Yes, I did."

"She's really nice, isn't she?"

"Yes, she's nice. I think we've talked about this before. I've got to go back to work. See you at supper time. And make sure you do your homework as soon as you get to Darlene's."

"I don't get homework. I'm only in grade one."

"Well, maybe I should tell your teacher to give you some."

"Does that mean you're gonna talk to Miss Klassen again soon?"

Josh tried not to laugh. "No, I was just kidding. Now go play with your friends. See you later."

Bradley rushed out the door into the school ground, and Josh waved to Melissa on his way out the door.

As he drove back to work, he thought about how cute it was that Bradley liked Melissa so much. For a little kid, Bradley had good taste in women, unlike himself.

Maybe he could learn something from the kid.

❧

Melissa walked from desk to desk during the class's free time, assisting her young students with the tasks in front of them. She worried that after such a large high-fat lunch Bradley might be sleepy, but she found him at his desk all alone, diligently working on tracing alphabet letters in his workbook.

She joined him, making herself as comfortable as possible, sitting beside him on one of the child-sized chairs in order to speak to him privately.

Bradley didn't look up at her. Instead, he concentrated

intently on making a pattern of dots and dashes in alternating colors on each letter, a very time-consuming project considering that all she wanted the children to do was to trace the letters to get used to their shapes. Still, it was a better alternative than staring out the window, which she had caught him doing many times since his parents went away.

"Hi, Bradley. Those are nice colors you're using."

"Thanks," he mumbled as he carefully chose the next color for his next dot.

"So, did you like church on Sunday?"

"Yeah," he muttered. "It was okay."

"Your uncle Josh says that he's going to take you and your brothers to Boys Club on Wednesday. He's going to go to the adult group, and Cleo is going to stay home."

"Mmmm," he mumbled as he carefully snapped on the lid and chose his next color.

"Do you like Cleo?"

Bradley nodded as he compared two red felt pens, then selected the one on the right.

"Does Cleo play with you?"

"Yes, except she kisses me too much when she does."

Melissa thought it good that Cleo was affectionate to the boys, except that made her think about Cleo kissing Josh. The thought turned her stomach, and she forced herself to think of something else.

Since Cleo obviously liked the children, it would make sense for her to participate in some of the children's school activities, with or without Josh. She knew many of the mothers from past years and wondered if Cleo would have any distinguishing features that would help Melissa identify her as having been at the recent science fair.

"I was wondering, what does Cleo look like?"

He closed one eye and stuck out his tongue to curl at the corner of his mouth as he concentrated on a series of dots on the next letter. His reply came out only as a mumble. "Uncle Josh says she's too fat. But I think she's okay."

Melissa tried not to cringe as she sucked in her stomach and covered it with one hand. "I think it's time to start packing up. It's almost story circle time."

For the rest of the day, Melissa could only half concentrate on the stories as Bradley's words echoed through her head. Fortunately, the day went quickly. She went straight home, but her thoughts kept drifting to Josh.

Children usually spoke with blunt honesty, yet she couldn't see the kind man she'd thought Josh to be speaking in such an unkind way in front of the children. It didn't matter if Cleo was overweight or not; it wasn't right to say it in front of them. As well, it bothered her to know Josh didn't care that Cleo wasn't going to Bible study with him, and, as well, it didn't seem like he expected Cleo would ever go to church with them. He never mentioned her once in the entire time they were together at the restaurant. Bradley had been the only one to ask if they should bring any food home for Cleo, and Josh had merely said no, that he didn't do doggie bags.

She didn't know much, but she did know that something was very wrong about the whole situation.

Melissa continued to stew about it but could come up with no answers.

By the time she'd finished supper, she was going crazy.

She wanted to talk to Cleo to see if she could discover what was going on in their relationship. If Josh wasn't going to take her hint about the couples' counseling sessions, then perhaps she could somehow get to know Cleo and convince her to convince Josh to participate, for the better of the two of them.

Phoning the McMillian household seemed like a good way to start.

The phone rang only once before someone picked it up. One of the boys answered, but she couldn't tell who it was.

Melissa cleared her throat. "Hi, this is Miss Klassen. Is that Ryan?"

"No, it's Kyle. Is Bradley in trouble?"

Melissa grinned. There was no shortage of sibling rivalry in the McMillian household. "No, he's not in trouble. I was wondering. Where's Cleo?"

"Cleo's outside. Do you want to talk to Uncle Josh?"

She didn't want to talk to Josh, but it was too late to do anything else as she heard the shuffle of the phone being passed.

"Hi, Melissa. What can I do for you?"

"Our class is having a field trip to the bakery next week, and I'm calling for drivers."

"Oh, and you're calling me because I've got a van? But I have to work, and I don't have any time off coming."

Since he made no offer to give the van to Cleo to let her drive, and since she didn't know if Cleo had her own car, Melissa decided to let that idea drop. "That's okay. I had to ask."

Melissa didn't know how it happened, but instead of ending the conversation, they ended up talking and talking until Josh suddenly noticed that it was past the younger boys' bedtime. After they hung up, Melissa couldn't remember the last time she'd spent an hour on the phone like that, even with her best friend. Josh was funny and kind and very interesting to talk to. She'd enjoyed every minute of their conversation, with one exception.

She still hadn't learned anything about Cleo.

But tomorrow was another day.

ஐ

"Hello again, Uncle Josh."

Josh sighed and looked up at the clock on the classroom wall. He had exactly twelve minutes to get back to work. If he caught all the lights green, he could do the drive in sixteen. He forced himself to smile. "Hi, Miss Klassen. I have no idea how his juice got spilled again. I checked the lid this morning. I really did. Twice."

As Bradley dug into the hamburger and fries, Melissa discreetly tilted her head to one side, indicating she wanted to speak to him privately. Instead of running back out the door, he approached her, then stood between Melissa and Bradley so Bradley couldn't hear her or see her mouth as she spoke.

Her voice dropped to a husky whisper. "This is two days in a row this week, and it's only Tuesday, plus this same thing happened on Friday. I wonder if he's doing it on purpose to get the hamburger and fries instead of a sandwich."

Josh quickly glanced over his shoulder at Bradley, who was shoveling the fries into his mouth three at a time. "I don't know. This time I'm only on my lunch break, not on a test drive, so I don't have time to stay and discuss it with you. I'll have to have a little sit-down with him tonight."

He turned to Bradley. "I've got to get back to work, Sport. See you at supper time."

Bradley stopped eating and looked up at him, his mouth still stuffed full of fries. He swallowed with great difficulty before speaking. "Aren't you going to stay and talk to Miss Klassen?"

"Not today—I'm going to be late. I just get half an hour for lunch, and it takes me more than that to drive back and forth."

"Oh."

"Bye, Sport, Miss Klassen."

With a quick nod, he strode out of the school building and back to the van. The entire way back to work, he could only question why he'd been to the school at lunchtime three days in a row.

Quite honestly, he didn't know what to do. He'd thought all the boys were adjusting well to their parents being gone, as well as accepting him in his new position of authority when he moved into their home. But now Bradley appeared to be making some kind of play for attention. Either that or he was challenging Josh in some way Josh couldn't understand. As much as he could tell, it started when the dog attacked him.

Immediately following the incident, he hadn't been worried about long-term trauma effects because he'd thought Bradley had handled it fine, and he had dismissed it. However, Bradley now seemed to be having some kind of delayed reaction. He didn't want to contemplate that the attack by the dog triggered some kind of latent stress anxiety about his parents having to go away.

He prayed that wasn't the case, because admittedly, Josh didn't know a lot about kids, nor did he know anyone who did. The few married friends he had, hadn't been married long. Of those who had been married for more than a few years, only a couple of them had kids, and they were still babies. The person he knew who had the most contact with kids was Theresa, but she was the last person he could ask as that would open a still very raw wound.

The only person he could think of who would have practical experience about behavioral problems with children would be Melissa, but he wasn't sure that asking the boy's teacher was appropriate. On the other hand, she'd told him he could call if he ever needed help, and this was definitely such a situation. The trouble was, he didn't know how to approach her. He'd seen or spoken to her at least once every day since Thursday, and he feared she could already be sick of seeing him—and he didn't want that to happen. He didn't know why he cared, but he did.

This time Rick did notice him arriving back late from lunch, forcing him to explain that he was having trouble with one of the kids. To his surprise Rick not only understood but shared many of his own fatherhood experiences from when his kids were younger. Unfortunately, all Rick did was tell what he thought were amusing stories, none of which helped Josh with Bradley's problem. While Rick talked and laughed at his own jokes, Josh sat and listened politely to his boss, thinking of how far behind he was getting on the repair roster.

When he finally managed to escape and get back to work, Josh prayed for an opportunity to talk to Melissa in an atmosphere where he didn't have the kids listening or, even better, when he didn't have to keep one eye on the time.

five

Melissa had been anticipating the class's free project time all day. Just like yesterday, most of the children scrambled to the fun areas first, but Bradley worked quietly at his desk with his printing workbook.

Again, she pulled one of the child-sized chairs beside him and lowered herself into it.

"Hi, Bradley. I see you're working at your printing. Do you like printing?"

"Mmm," he muttered as he carefully printed a series of the letter J.

Melissa smiled. Today's class project had been printing the names of every member of every child's family. Bradley had included his mother's and father's names as well as his uncle Josh. He'd had difficulty getting the J straight and was now practicing a series of very fine-looking Js. Altogether with his brothers, Bradley's family consisted of eight names including his own, making Bradley's list the longest of all his classmates.

One thing she had noticed, Cleo's name did not appear on Bradley's list.

"That's good work on your uncle Josh's name. Do you think you'd like to add Cleo to your list?"

Bradley stopped printing. "Cleo? But she's not in my family."

"Still, she lives with you in your house, doesn't she?"

"Well, yes, I guess so."

"Then don't you think she belongs on the list?"

He broke out into a wide smile. "Yes. I like Cleo really lots. Did you know that sometimes she even sleeps with me?"

Melissa smiled back. Despite an improper relationship with Josh, it seemed Cleo was making an effort to fit in with the family. "That's great, Bradley."

"Most of the time Uncle Josh says Cleo sleeps in her own bed, but sometimes when I have to get up in the night, I peek into Uncle Josh's room and see her sleeping in Uncle Josh's bed." His voice dropped to a whisper. "But don't tell Uncle Josh I told you that."

Bradley grinned, but Melissa thought she might throw up. She hadn't wanted to know that.

"Do you have a dog, Miss Klassen? I was at your house, remember? But I didn't see a dog."

"No, I don't have a dog."

"But you have a car, right?"

She couldn't believe the direction of their conversation, but if he said something that could give her a glimpse into what was bothering him so much that he'd called his uncle to the school three days in a row, Melissa planned to listen.

"Yes, I have a car."

"Does it run good? Uncle Josh is a really good mechanic. Before my mom and dad left, our van made some funny noises, but Uncle Josh fixed it all up." He paused to grin. "Me and Kyle got to help."

"That's 'Kyle and I got to help.' "

"Did you help Uncle Josh fix the van too? I never saw you at our house. Kyle never told me."

Melissa shook her head. "No, I didn't help your uncle Josh fix your van."

"How is your car? Does it ever make funny noises?"

"Sometimes, I suppose. But I think all cars do when they're cold."

He nodded knowingly, and Melissa smiled at the future budding mechanic, imagining Josh tutoring the boys on the fine art of spark plugs and oil changes. She had no idea how the conversation changed from Cleo to her car, but she had run out of time to ask more questions without Bradley figuring out what she was trying to do.

"I think it's time for story circle."

The rest of the afternoon progressed in a blur of activity, allowing no time to speak with Bradley in relative privacy again. When the final bell of the day rang, Bradley dashed out the door with the rest of his classmates, so Melissa tidied up, as she did every day, and went home.

With no plans for the evening, Melissa settled onto the couch after supper, all prepared to watch a little television, when the doorbell rang.

Before she opened the door, she peeked through the mini-blinds to see an increasingly familiar blue minivan parked on the street.

She ran to the door. "Josh? What are you doing here? Is something wrong?"

He smiled, and her heart made a foolish little flutter.

"I'm not sure. I'm here to see what we can do about your car."

Melissa blinked and tried not to let her mouth hang open. "My car? There's nothing wrong with my car."

Josh's smile dropped. "Bradley said your car was making strange noises, and you needed someone to fix it."

"But. . ." She let her voice trail off, then lowered her head and pinched the bridge of her nose with her forefinger and thumb. "We were talking this afternoon, and he asked me if my car ever made funny noises. So I said it sometimes made funny noises when it's cold. But all cars do."

"Well, not really. Do you want me to have a look at it anyway?"

She tried to smile. "I don't think that's necessary, but thanks for asking. Since you've come all this way, I hate for it to be for nothing. Would you like to come in and have coffee?"

He didn't move, but instead stood in the doorway and checked his wristwatch. "I guess I could. Tyler is baby-sitting his brothers, and I told him I'd be about an hour. I'm probably safe to stay for coffee. Thanks."

He followed her through the living room and into the kitchen, making her very glad she'd done the dishes before relaxing. She set about measuring the coffee while Josh sat down at the kitchen table.

When she finished, she turned around to see Josh smiling, his gaze somewhat unfocused. As soon as he noticed her looking at him, he sat back in the chair and crossed his arms over his chest, not losing the smile. "It's so quiet in here. I'd almost forgotten what it was like."

"They can't be going strong twenty-four hours a day. Surely your house is quiet at night."

"That's true, but by the time Tyler goes to bed, I have to rush around getting things ready for the next day, and then I'm so tired, I just fall into bed. I never knew this was going to be so much work."

Melissa pulled out the other chair and positioned herself across the table from him. "I can't imagine adding five boys to my family overnight."

"They're not that bad, really. It's kinda nice, in some ways."

A comfortable silence remained in the kitchen while Melissa poured two cups of coffee and slid one across the table to Josh. He sipped the hot brew slowly, closing his eyes while he did so. Watching him let himself be so relaxed in her presence made her feel peaceful too.

He held the mug below his chin and smiled lazily. "I think I've figured it out. Bradley has a crush on you."

Melissa sputtered into her coffee. "A crush on me?"

Josh nodded. "You should hear him. He's always singing your praises, telling me about what a good teacher you are and how nice you are. And now this, sending me over here to fix your car when there's nothing wrong with it. He wants to do something special for you."

She could feel her cheeks heat up. "I don't know. I don't want to sound arrogant or anything, but other little boys have had crushes on me as their teacher before, and he's not acting the same."

"But not all kids are the same. I'm learning the hard way how different kids can be, even in the same family. I wouldn't have believed it until I moved in with them. Sometimes it's hard to believe they're even related."

She couldn't help her grin. "I don't know. Being with all of you together on Sunday, you all look very related to me. Everyone has the same hair, even you. And all of you have the same chin. All of you have brown eyes too, except for the oldest boy, Tyler, is it? It was actually quite amusing."

His grin changed to a very engaging, roguish smile. "Yeah. Us McMillians are all handsome louts, aren't we?"

"Oh, puh-leeze."

Instead of responding, he continued to smile brazenly, and then he winked.

Melissa cleared her throat. "When Ryan was in grade one, I remember meeting their father, and as I recall, you two look a lot alike. He's quite a bit older than you, though."

"Yes. Brian is thirteen years older than me. I was Mom and Dad's little 'surprise.' "

Melissa turned to look out the window, wondering if all the McMillians were prone to giving out more information than she needed to know. "You have no other brothers or sisters?"

"No, it's just the two of us left now. Mom and Dad died five years ago."

"Oh, I'm sorry. Please tell me if this is none of my business, but how come your nephews have never been to church in their lives? Isn't your brother a Christian?"

"No. I was the only Christian in my family. I started going to youth group with my friends and came to know the Lord through them. By that time Brian was married and gone and already had kids, and my parents wouldn't listen to me. Every day, I wish I had tried harder to show them God's love and His wish for their salvation."

"Don't do that to yourself; don't dwell on something that can't be changed. I'm sure you did your best at the time. I think it's great that you're trying to show the gospel to your nephews now. You can really make a difference in their lives."

"I hope so. Until now, I've been praying about what would be the best way to introduce God into their lives. So far I've just started telling them as often as I can how God loves them, and now I think is a good time to start explaining about Jesus and why His sacrifice was necessary. I don't know if they really believe they're all little sinners, but believe me, they are." He gave a halfhearted laugh. "I hope and pray that I can answer their questions. Actually, I hope they have questions because that's going to be the only way I know they're thinking about it—and not letting everything I say go in one ear and out the other. I guess you know what that's like, being a teacher and all."

She nodded and smiled, and thought of what a good decision it had been for Josh's brother to leave him in charge of the children. Josh truly wanted the best for his nephews, both physically by taking care of their obvious needs, but also, he was doing his best to see to their spiritual development and, ultimately, their salvation. She could tell how much he loved them and that they loved him back.

Josh McMillian was a very nice man. Not for the first time, she wished she had met him another way instead of their current and rather convoluted parent-teacher association.

Melissa immediately closed the lid on her thoughts. It wasn't right for her to feel that way about him, not just because he was the acting parent of one of her students. Despite the impropriety of his living arrangements with Cleo, he was taken.

She sipped her coffee to help get her thoughts back to where they should have been in the first place. "Yes, sometimes it's hard to know what is really sinking in, especially with younger children. Sometimes you don't think they're paying attention, and then they prove you wrong at the oddest and most inopportune times by repeating what you've said, sometimes almost word for word."

"That's something else I'm finding out the hard way. I'm hoping they're all being honest with me. I asked them all what they thought of church, and they said it was okay, because that opened up the door for me to talk to them about how God loves them all as individuals. That's why I think this is a good time to buy them each their own Bible. I stopped off at the Christian bookstore last night on my way home from work, and I couldn't believe how many there were for kids. It occurred to me that there's a big difference in their reading levels, and I don't know anything about that kind of thing. Bradley can't read anything except for his name and a couple of short words, Kyle only reads books where something is getting blown up, and Ryan is somewhere in the middle. Tyler of course can read at adult level, but his brain just isn't there. He's fifteen, and it seems that despite his ability, all he reads are comics. Andrew will read anything, and he studies all the time, when he's not on the computer, which kind of scares me at times. He's the exact opposite of Tyler."

Josh stopped to suck in a deep breath. "All Tyler can think about is turning sixteen and getting his driver's license, but I don't want to go there."

Melissa smiled at his mock horror, which maybe wasn't totally pretending. "I can only guess."

"I was wondering if you could help me get something age appropriate for each one of them."

"Sure, I could do that. What grades are they all in?"

She watched as Josh closed one eye and started counting on his fingers as he spoke. "Let's see, you know Bradley is in grade one. Ryan is in grade three, which means Kyle is in grade five. Andrew is in grade eight, and Tyler is in high school, I think grade ten or eleven. I sometimes forget."

"That's quite a spread. Still, I don't think we'll have any trouble picking something out for them at their own levels. When would be a good time for you to go shopping?"

"Tomorrow I have to be home right after work because I'm going to take them to the Boys Clubs you told me about, and Tyler wants to take his girlfriend to youth group, so I'll have to get started making supper as soon as I get home. Thursday is swimming lessons and Cub Scouts, so that's out. I can't ask you to go shopping on Friday night. I'm sure you have better things to do then, so I guess that leaves Saturday, if I can convince Tyler to watch his brothers for awhile. I'm definitely not taking that rowdy bunch into a bookstore. I once thought I was doing a good thing by taking them all to the library. Never again. Have you ever been kicked out of a library? It's really embarrassing."

Melissa didn't think she wanted to go there, either. "I'm actually not busy Friday night, but I think Saturday would probably be a better time for you. Let's pencil in Saturday."

Josh sipped the last of the coffee. "Saturday, then. I think I'd better get going. Are you sure you don't want me to have a look at your car?"

"You drove my car Thursday night, remember? Did you think there might have been anything wrong with it then? I assure you nothing has changed."

"Of course. But I had to ask. After all, I'll have to give an account of my lack of fixing your car to Bradley. And speaking of Bradley, I sure hope he doesn't play games with his lunch again tomorrow. We had a little talk about that."

She smiled, thinking of Bradley's concern for her and her car as she led Josh to the door. "I'm sure Bradley will start behaving now that you've talked to him, and you know what he's up to. I'll see you Saturday, I guess."

❧

Josh could tell by the number of cars parked on the street and in the driveway that he was at the right house. Most of all, he could tell because Melissa's car was one of them.

She had said that the majority of the attendees at this particular study were single adults, some single parents, and some just plain old single. He couldn't tell which category he fit into, but the bottom line was "single." In the back of his mind, he had hoped that Melissa would be attending this study as well, because as far as he could tell, she was single too.

He'd phoned her when he got home from work to ask for directions since he was fairly new in the neighborhood, and to both his surprise and hers, before they realized it, they'd spent half an hour on the phone. They'd talked about many things, starting with Bradley's day at school, but after that their conversation wandered to other areas, nothing in particular of note, just a friendly conversation between friends.

But was she a friend? He didn't know how other parents talked to their kids' teachers because he'd only been a parent for a month and had no experience with kids or teachers. When he was a kid, he'd been far from the ideal student, and his teachers were the last people he ever wanted to talk to. Back then, he hadn't even thought of teachers as real, normal people.

Now as a quasi-parent, he would have liked to compare notes on dealing with school issues with his friends, but none of his friends had kids in school yet. Besides, since he'd moved into his brother's house, he hadn't had time to see a single one of his friends. All he had to go on were the pages of notes he'd made when he talked to Brian and Sasha before they left, which certainly didn't encompass specifically dealing with teachers as people.

Somewhere along the line, Melissa had crossed over from being merely Bradley's teacher to something else he couldn't quite define.

It was obvious she liked kids, or else she wouldn't be a teacher. She'd apparently taken an extra liking to Bradley, which probably wasn't a difficult thing. Melissa had a warm heart and a sensitive nature which drew her naturally to Bradley because of his unusual family situation. And being so inclined to help the helpless, that also included him in his adventure into instant parenthood. He didn't know who needed more help with life, Bradley or himself. He refused to be embarrassed about it, though. He was mature enough to know when he was in over his head and needed help.

Taking the kids to the Wednesday night church activities had been a great suggestion. At first Bradley had been hesitant about going to the Boys Club, and Andrew hadn't wanted to go at all, which Josh found very discouraging in light of their enthusiasm about attending church last Sunday. Then when Josh mentioned that he wanted to go to the adult meeting and that he might be seeing Melissa there, thankfully, Bradley changed his mind. Bradley had then proceeded to convince Andrew that Boys Club would be fun.

His surge of joy at the thought of going to the Bible study meeting was immediately followed by a sinking feeling of dread that he wouldn't know anyone there if Melissa didn't go, and he didn't know how to deal with it. Up until recently, he'd never known what it was like to be alone. He certainly never had any time to himself since he moved into his brother's house. Whether the house was quiet or when he was out, he spent his time either running some errand he had to do with the kids or thinking of something he had to do with them or for them. Tonight marked the first time since he took responsibility for them that he had an evening just for himself, if he didn't count having to drive them to the church for the Boys Club and youth group.

Laughter drifting from inside the house brought Josh's thoughts back to what he was doing. Rather than stand forever at the door and look like an idiot, he gathered his nerve and knocked.

A man whom Josh didn't remember seeing at church on Sunday answered. Josh didn't know if he was the host or if he was just being polite and answering the door.

"Welcome! If you're here for the Bible study, please come in."

A quick glance through the people present confirmed what he dreaded. He didn't recognize a single person there. It had been so long since he'd gone anywhere he didn't already know someone, at least by face, that he didn't know what to do.

He was about to quietly take a seat in the corner when Melissa appeared from around the hall corner.

"Josh! I'm so glad you could come. Come here and let me introduce you."

Josh smiled weakly. He didn't know what was wrong with him. He'd never been shy before, at least not as an adult.

Being so proved that he'd become too dependent on having Theresa at his side, and he'd spent too much time doing only what was comfortable.

Now, in the space of a short month, nothing in his life was comfortable or familiar. He'd jumped in without knowing what he was doing to look after the boys. He'd moved into his brother's house and had to deal with all that went with moving into an unfamiliar neighborhood, which also included leaving the church he'd attended for the past six years. At the same time, he suddenly found himself single again. The only thing that hadn't changed was his job, but that was just a job, nothing of true personal value. If he turned in his notice, no one would really care. They would just hire someone else.

For the first time in his adult life, and for the first time since he could remember, there was no one he could talk to; he had no friend who could truly understand how he felt. For the first time ever, he felt alone.

With a gentle touch of her warm hand on his arm, Melissa directed Josh to a couple who included the man who answered the door. "This is Mike and Patty Flannigan, and they are our hosts. Patty is also our church secretary."

Josh extended his hand to Mike. "Pleased to meet you both."

Mike nodded and returned the handshake. "Same. I've never seen you before. Are you new to our church?"

Josh smiled. The church was only one in a long list of things he was new to. "Yes, I am."

"Great. I hope you like it here. Now if you'll excuse me, I think someone else has just arrived."

Melissa introduced him around to everyone present, but by the time he'd been introduced to at least fifteen people, he knew he'd be lucky to remember more than a few names by the end of the evening.

He enjoyed the study thoroughly, both in reading and learning from God's Word. In addition to that, he also appreciated relating to other adults in a social setting that had nothing to do with children or what was wrong with their cars.

The whole time, Melissa sat beside him like they'd come together, which they hadn't. She treated him with a familiarity that would have indicated to everyone present that a friendship existed when there was none beyond the minimal connection they'd established through Bradley. He appreciated her thoughtfulness from the bottom of his heart.

At precisely 8:30 everyone who was a parent filed out to pick up their kids, while the singles and those without children gathered around the dining room table, which had been set out with a coffee urn and a plate of cookies.

Josh felt he belonged with both groups, yet he belonged with neither.

His responsibilities directed his choice, and Melissa escorted him to the door.

She stepped close to him, speaking softly so no one else could hear her words. "I'm glad you could come. Up until the last minute, I wasn't sure you were going to make it."

He sighed, rested his hand on the doorknob, and then backed away to talk without being in the way of anyone else leaving. "I know. Ryan couldn't find one of his shoes. We finally found it in the corner of the kitchen."

"I guess Cleo is at home all alone right now, waiting for you all to get back."

Josh checked his watch. "Yeah. I think after the younger kids are in bed and just Tyler is up, we'll go out for a short walk." Josh turned to Melissa and smiled. "But just a short one. I've got to get up early for work in the morning. I'm really tired, but sometimes it's nice to get away from it all, and it seems lately the only chance I get to do that is when I take Cleo out."

"Oh."

He checked his watch a second time. "I guess I should go. See you Saturday? You know, to go to the Christian bookstore?"

Her answering smile seemed strangely sad, and Josh couldn't figure out what he'd said or done to cause the change.

"Yes, I'll see you Saturday."

six

"Uncle Josh? I think you'd better phone Miss Klassen."

Josh hung his keys on the hook beside the door and sat on the bottom step leading to the kitchen to yank off his work boots. "What time did she call? Did she say what she wanted?"

Being so close to the floor, he sat pretty much at eye level with Bradley, giving him a good opportunity to study the boy.

Bradley wouldn't make eye contact. Instead, he pushed a few particles of sand around on the linoleum with his toe, watching it intently as he spoke. "Well, she didn't really call. I was talking to her at school today, and she sounded kinda sad. I think you should go talk to her or something."

He opened his mouth, about to tell Bradley that whatever was making his teacher sad was unfortunate but none of his business, but he snapped it back shut again. Last night as he left the Bible study meeting, he'd seen a sadness in her eyes that he hadn't noticed until right that minute. He couldn't even remember what they'd been talking about that might have made her sad. As best he recalled, he'd been babbling on about taking the dog for a walk when he got home that night.

"What were the two of you talking about at school?"

Finally, Bradley made eye contact, and he could see the truth shining in Bradley's eyes. "Nuthin, really. I was just telling her about how Cleo kisses me and everyone else when we get home, but she kisses you most of all. Do you think she's sad because she doesn't have a dog? I asked her before if she had a dog, and she said no, she just has a car."

"Not everyone can have a dog, Bradley. A dog is a lot of work and a big responsibility."

"How about a puppy, then? A puppy is littler than a dog. Do you think she'd like a puppy?"

Josh bit his bottom lip to keep from smiling. When Cleo was a pup she'd eaten untold shoes, never two from the same pair, dug holes all over his yard, plus she'd dug up a few of his neighbor's flowers. Cleo's favorite chew toys as a pup were things made of wood, such as the legs of his wooden kitchen chairs. He remembered having to make an emergency trip to the vet when Cleo chewed part of a blackberry bush and got a thorn stuck in her gums.

He cleared his throat and rested one hand on Bradley's shoulder. "I don't think Miss Klassen wants a puppy. But if you think she wants me to, I can certainly phone and talk to her."

Bradley's face lit up like a Christmas tree. "That's great, Uncle Josh! Are you going to phone her right now?"

"I think I'll wait until after supper. She's probably eating right now."

"Would you like to have supper with Miss Klassen? Men and ladies do that all the time. You know, like at a restaurant. You can talk way better there." He shuffled closer. "You know. With no kids."

Josh wondered where Bradley came up with that line but decided he probably heard it from Brian and Sasha, as they would have required many private conversations in order to make the difficult decisions concerning her care and treatment.

He wondered if Bradley knew that it was a different thing for married couples to go out to talk in private than for two single adults to go out to a restaurant for dinner. For married couples, it was simply getting away from the kids, but what Bradley was suggesting for two single adults was otherwise known as a date.

Part of him thought it would be a good idea. It had been a long time since he'd been in the dating scene. He'd gone steady with Theresa for three years. He even thought they would one day get married. Since they'd progressed that far in their relationship, it had been a long time since he'd considered going out with Theresa being a date. On the other hand, if he went out to a restaurant with Melissa, that would be called a date.

He thought of what it would be like to date Melissa. Every time they'd talked, either in person or on the phone, which had been in a number of varied circumstances, they'd had very pleasant conversations and he'd thoroughly enjoyed himself. In different circumstances, he could really like her.

Josh stood and looked down at Bradley. Right in front of him was part of the reason that the more sensible and responsible side of him knew that dating Melissa or anyone else was something he shouldn't do.

As much as it hurt, Theresa had been right when she pointed out to him that no woman in her right mind would want to go out with him when he was caring for five active boys. And, if he ever found a woman who could find joy in such mayhem, everything would change when Brian and Sasha returned. Their projected "best" return date was eighteen months, only one of which had passed.

He had his personal doubts about Sasha being a best-case scenario. The worst-case scenario would be that it could take years, maybe never. So far, he'd agreed that if Sasha didn't get better in three years, they would reevaluate their strategy for him caring for the boys. Brian and Sasha couldn't stay in Switzerland forever.

That being the case, he suspected he would have the boys for at least three years. Three years was also the amount of time he'd been going out with Theresa—a reasonable time, he thought, to decide that marriage was the next step in a relationship. In their case, it hadn't been. When his situation changed, so did their relationship. It was suddenly over.

If he did find someone who wouldn't mind five kids being part of the package along with him, whenever his time with them was up, everything would change. When that happened, he wouldn't be the same person as he was today or even the same person as he was with the kids in his care. To suddenly have them yanked away and placed back with their parents would be a big transition in his life. He suspected that moving out would be more difficult than the process of moving in. Already he dreaded it, because he knew he'd miss them. On the other hand, if Sasha didn't get better and needed to be institutionalized or required care herself, that would mean he would probably have to help his brother raise the kids until the youngest became a teenager.

Either way, his life was in limbo, and it wasn't fair to drag a woman into such a complex situation.

All things considered, it was wrong to start something he couldn't finish. With any woman, he would have to make it plain from the first date that he had no intention of developing a solid relationship. If such an arrangement was acceptable, that wouldn't be the kind of person he would want to date in the first place. He valued friendships and other relationships too much to have a quick fling, which would be all a date without any intention of furthering the relationship would be. Nor did he want to be anyone else's quick fling.

Josh gave his head a mental shake. He didn't know why he was thinking of such things in the first place. He didn't have time to date, even if he was inclined to do so. He had to schedule time and make special arrangements to take his dog for a twenty-minute walk. Every minute of every day was filled with his job, caring for the kids, housework, and running errands which included either doing things for them or driving them halfway across the galaxy or anything else in between.

He'd heard jokes from the parents of older kids at his old church about being "Mom's Taxi" but he'd never fully understood them. Now that he was experiencing it, the joke wasn't very funny. The only reason he'd managed to take the time for himself to go to the Bible study meeting was because he'd dropped them all off at the same place for activities that started at the same time.

"Uncle Josh? I can help you make spaghetti, and then you can phone Miss Klassen sooner. Right?"

Josh forced himself to smile. "Yes, that's right."

ॐ

"Hello?"

"Hi, Melissa. It's me, Josh."

Melissa's heart nearly stopped, and her words caught in her throat. Since the end of school, she hadn't been able to stop thinking about him.

For some reason Bradley had stayed in the classroom after the last bell. He said he wanted to talk to her, but all he did was tell her all about his uncle Josh. If she hadn't actually met the man, from everything Bradley had said, she would have thought Josh to be some form of super-being. Not only did Uncle Josh do the exalted job of fixing cars for a living, he cooked every meal including making all of their lunches every day, a procedure with a magnitude Melissa could only imagine. He also drove them everywhere, helped them all with their homework, and did most of the housework, although Bradley said he "made" everyone do something.

Not only did he also do the laundry, the Wonderful Uncle Josh managed to get the pink out of everyone's white socks, a story about which she didn't dare press for details.

The man even did all the grocery shopping, but he let the boys put everything away.

In all this, Melissa hadn't heard Cleo's name once. The only time Bradley mentioned Cleo was to say that she kissed Uncle Josh a lot.

Melissa couldn't begin to guess at the kind of relationship Josh and Cleo had, but the more she heard, the less she liked it. Today it bothered her so much she actually felt sick. So far, it seemed the only things Cleo did were kiss, sleep, and eat, apparently a lot. But for all she didn't do as a part of the household, Josh still appreciated her good qualities. It was more than obvious that he loved Cleo dearly, which said a lot about him as a person.

Nonetheless, the bottom line was that the relationship was very one-sided, and that was very wrong. In addition to that was the greater problem that they were living together without the covering of marriage.

There had to be something she could do.

"Melissa? Are you there? Are you okay?"

"Yes, I'm here. Sorry, I got distracted. Is something wrong? Can you not make it Saturday?"

"Nothing's wrong, and yes, I still have plans to go to the bookstore with you on Saturday. Is it a problem for you?"

"No, that's still fine for me."

Dead air space loomed over the phone lines.

She heard Josh clear his throat. "It occurred to me that I still haven't found a way to thank you properly for everything you did for Bradley. Since there's nothing wrong with your car, Bradley made a suggestion. We all agreed that we'd like to have you come over to our house for dinner tomorrow night. You'll get to meet Cleo too. Bradley says you've been asking about her."

Melissa felt her face turn ten shades of red, making her very glad Josh couldn't see her on the other end of the phone. "Oh, well, yes, I guess I have."

"If you need some time to think about it, that's fine. Take all the time you need. I just want to warn you, things are a little, uh, well, less formal here at home than in a restaurant."

She couldn't help but smile. Lunch at the restaurant had been an adventure in itself. She couldn't imagine six males at the same table where there were no restrictions or codes of decorum.

And since Josh asked, she had been praying for an opportunity to speak to Cleo. If she couldn't figure out how to get Cleo to come to her, then she had prayed for a way to go to Cleo. Now the chance had been laid in her lap. She couldn't turn it down, even if it wasn't exactly the way she thought it should be, or that the thought of actually meeting Cleo face-to-face scared her silly.

Melissa cleared her throat. "Yes, I'd like that. What time tomorrow?"

She smiled at the muffled sound of Josh putting his hand over the mouthpiece of the phone and whispering, "She said yes," to the boys. His voice then came through the phone loud and clear. "That's great. If you want to get a pen, I'll give you directions."

As she wrote everything down, her smile dropped as what she was about to do started to sink in.

This was it. She was going to meet Cleo. She had no idea what she was going to say or do, but she did know one thing. Instead of sleeping tonight, Melissa would be praying like she'd never prayed before.

❧

Melissa sucked in a deep, deep breath, steeled her nerve, and began the seemingly endless walk up Josh's brother's sidewalk.

Rather than drive herself crazy, she refused to think about meeting Cleo. Instead she forced herself to think about what Josh might be cooking for supper. Bradley had assured her countless times of the quality of his uncle's cooking skills, although the only dish he ever seemed to mention was spaghetti. She couldn't remember the last time she'd made dinner for eight people, if she ever had. Feeding a large group made her think of the potluck dinners her church had every once in awhile, except that with Josh and the boys, every day would be a potluck. She didn't know what he would be able to cook in such massive quantities every day. She didn't even know what the average single man knew how to cook in the first place. If it were her feeding a large group on short notice, she would probably make. . .spaghetti.

Today at school she had taken Bradley aside first thing in the morning and asked him to please keep the fact that she was going to his house for supper just between them and not to mention it to anyone, not even his best friend. Knowing children as she did, she had been careful not to use the word "secret." If she had, it would have quickly become a bulletin through the entire school population by the time recess ended.

He hadn't understood why she didn't want anyone to know, so she did her best to explain it in a way that a six year old would understand, telling him that if the principal found out, she could get in trouble. The trouble was, she wasn't lying. Her only course of defense would be that she had accepted Josh's invitation to give the incident with the dog closure.

Following Bradley's agreement not to say anything, he had broken into a gleeful smile. He told her that they hadn't had dessert at home since Uncle Josh moved in, but he'd heard Uncle Josh talking to Cleo about making something. Bradley proceeded to tell her about his mother's chocolate cake and how a whole cake never lasted until bedtime, even if the first piece wasn't cut until supper.

The concept of raising five boys was so mind-boggling that Melissa wondered if part of Bradley's mother's illness needing such drastic treatment in a faraway place had a lot to do with mental stress.

She had been about to ask Bradley a question about what Josh and Cleo were going to make when Bradley started talking again. He told her how he heard Uncle Josh doing something in the kitchen after he and the other two younger boys were in bed while Tyler and Cleo went for a walk.

The concept that a woman wouldn't even help with company coming for dinner made Melissa both sick and angry.

Now if she could only release that anger, she would be able to talk to Cleo and Josh in love as a Christian sister.

Melissa stood outside the door, counted to ten, and raised her fist to knock. Before she made the second rap, frantic barking increased in volume, ending with thumping and scratching against the door.

Children squealed and yelled; the blow-'em-up sounds of a video game went suddenly dead, followed by a mad scramble on the other side of the door, along with more barking.

Suddenly, the noise on the other side of the door went completely silent, and the door flew open. The three youngest boys stood neatly in a row, smiling ear to ear at her. Andrew and Tyler stood behind them, and Josh stood off to the side, half standing and half leaning as he held back a frantic tan-colored dog. The little grouping almost made Melissa wish she had a camera.

She smiled at them all. "Hi."

Josh's warm smile did funny things to her insides, but she convinced herself it was just hunger.

"Hi to you too," he said, his deep voice coming out with a skip as his dog made another frantic lunge that made his whole body jerk with the movement. "I hope you like dogs."

"Yes, I like dogs."

"In that case, brace yourself." Josh released the dog, who immediately leapt toward her. "Melissa, meet Cleo."

Melissa froze. "Cleo?" She braced herself so the impact of two huge paws on her stomach wouldn't knock her over, and before she could gather her thoughts, a wet, rough tongue washed her face.

seven

Josh felt his stomach take a nosedive. He had expected Cleo to jump on Melissa, but he hadn't expected the dog to go so far as to kiss her in the face or jump so hard that she almost knocked Melissa over.

He quickly squeezed his way past the boys and dragged Cleo down and away.

"I'm really sorry, Melissa. She doesn't usually kiss strangers. Just us."

His stomach clenched even more as he watched Melissa wipe her mouth with the back of her hand, then brush off the spots where Cleo's feet had been on her clothing. "It's okay," she mumbled. "Cleo just wasn't who, er, what I was expecting."

"I know what you mean. I'll admit she's not very well trained, and she's kind of chunky for a yellow Lab, but I've been making sure that she gets a walk every day, even if it's just Tyler taking her out for a short one in the evening when I don't have time. She's actually lost a little weight recently."

Ryan's voice piped up behind him. "No, she hasn't, Uncle Josh."

"She has so," Andrew replied.

"She's not fat!" Bradley said, running to hug Cleo as he spoke. "It's not her fault."

"No, it's your fault for leaving food on the coffee table," Kyle taunted.

"Is not!"

"Pizza isn't good for dogs, you know."

"Yeah, she could get sick on it, and that would be all your fault."

"It's the chili you left on the table that made her barf, Stupid."

"You're the one who didn't clean up the dishes when you were supposed to. That was your fault."

"You're the one who let her knock the glass over and get broken!"

"Yeah, she almost cut her foot, you know. That was your fault."

Josh waved one hand in the air to get everyone's attention, not exactly sure when he had lost control. "Boys! Boys! Let's settle down and let Miss Klassen go sit in the living room, okay?"

He turned to Melissa and forced himself to smile. "The living room is this way." He released Cleo, who trotted faithfully behind him like she was supposed to. "Have a seat. You want some coffee?"

"Only if it's made. Would you like some help?"

He glanced briefly in the direction of the kitchen. If she went in now she'd see the mess, and he didn't want that. Not that he'd been great at housekeeping before, but he had always prided himself on not being a total slob like some of the other single guys he knew. He couldn't believe how much he'd lowered his standards in the past month. "No, you're my guest. You stay here. I won't be long."

Josh hustled into the kitchen and dumped the frozen carrots into the boiling water, then added more water because he wasn't sure how long it had been boiling, and the water had gotten a bit low. He started the coffee while the water returned to a boil and then went back to the living room, but what he saw stopped him in the doorway.

Melissa sat in the center of the couch, surrounded by all the kids. Even Cleo lay sedately nestled at her feet. He didn't know what was so funny, but everyone was smiling. Even Tyler wore a grin from ear to ear. If Josh didn't know any better, he would have said that Cleo was smiling too.

Not that he was jealous, he was just sorry he missed out.

Only Cleo noticed him reenter the room, but when she stood and wagged her tail, everyone turned.

Melissa smiled at him as he sat in the chair on the other side of the room, since he couldn't get near the couch with the crowd around her. "I was just telling them that something sure smells good, and I'll bet it isn't spaghetti."

"Uh, no," he muttered, wondering why she thought he might serve spaghetti, because it was something he tended to make a lot.

"You know, it almost smells like turkey."

"Uh, it is turkey."

Her eyebrows raised, and her eyes went wide, which Josh thought rather cute. "Turkey? You made a turkey?"

He shrugged his shoulders. "It's really not a hard thing to cook a turkey. It's just like a big chicken. I took it out of the freezer last night when you said you would come, and all I did was stick it in the oven before I left for work and set the timer. I bought this great book that tells how long to cook things and all that stuff."

"I guess I'm only used to having turkey for special occasions when there are a lot of people to feed, but you have to feed a large group every day."

"Not really. Kyle and Bradley are still little. They only count as half a kid each."

"Uncle Josh!"

The two younger boys sprang from their places beside Melissa and jumped on top of him, poking Josh enough to make him defend himself, which he did by tickling them and poking them back until they squealed. The ruckus started Cleo barking, so he started to push away before everything got too carried away. "That's enough, guys. I think it's time to—"

"Dog pile!" shouted Ryan.

In a split second Ryan and Andrew were also on top of him, and he was helpless beneath the mass of small bodies.

He heard Tyler talking to Melissa. "This happens all the time. Don't worry, no one ever gets hurt."

"That's good," Melissa replied in a tiny voice.

At the sound of her voice, the kids suddenly remembered

they had company, scuffled off of Josh, and quietly returned to the couch, sitting perfectly still with their hands folded neatly in their laps as if nothing had ever happened.

Josh rose from the chair, which now felt rather lonely with four less people in it. He ran one hand down his shirt to smooth the wrinkles out of it, then ran his fingers through his tousled hair, knowing what he really needed now was a comb. "Anyway, I was going to say that it's great to cook a turkey during the week, because then there's leftovers for sandwiches, and if I figure out everything else right, I won't have to cook too much tomorrow."

"I suppose."

"If you'll excuse me, I'll go pour that coffee and get everything together. I know the boys will entertain you."

He'd barely stepped one foot into the kitchen when he heard Melissa's voice behind him. "Please, Josh. Let me help."

Josh's heart nearly stopped. He didn't know why, but he had wanted to impress her by showing her that he could do a good job looking after his nephews and cook a decent meal at the same time. After the scene at the front door, then the ruckus in the living room, his last hope for any semblance of respect would have been for him to put out a nice, organized supper. But now she'd seen the state of the kitchen.

As he turned around, Melissa stood in the doorway watching him with her head tilted to one side. "Surely there's something I can do. Can I mash potatoes or something? Slice the turkey? I want to help—there's so much to do."

She would get no argument from him there. Everything was cooked and ready to be dished up. With another adult in the kitchen, they could do it in half the time.

"I guess. Everybody's hungry, so the faster we get supper on the table, the better."

"I see you set the dining room table instead of eating in the kitchen."

The reason was so she wouldn't see the mess, but it was too late for that. He had wanted to impress her, although he didn't know why. It shouldn't have mattered, but it did.

Josh turned around and picked the oven mitts off the counter. "The dining room table is bigger," he mumbled.

As he turned his head, he caught Melissa peeking into one of the pots on the stove and poking the contents with a fork. "It looks like the potatoes are done. Would you like me to mash them?"

He felt his cheeks heating up. "Melissa, this feels so strange. How could I be the one to give you instructions on what to do? I thought I'd be okay with this, but I'm not. I feel strange giving a woman orders in the kitchen. Especially when you're supposed to be my guest. If I were a guest for dinner at your house, I would be sitting down and letting you do everything, and I wouldn't feel guilty. You shouldn't be doing this, but I'm not going to turn you down."

"Good. I was expecting hamburgers if you didn't make spaghetti. I certainly wasn't expecting a delicious meal like this."

Josh couldn't help himself. He grinned as he backed up with the turkey roaster and plunked it on top of the only empty spot he could find on the counter. "Don't say that until you've tasted it."

He removed the oven mitts, poured two cups of coffee, and started slicing the turkey while Melissa dished everything out. When they were almost done, he poked his head around the corner to call the boys, who dutifully came one after the other into the kitchen. Each of them carried a bowl or plate of food to the table without argument and sat down quietly, exactly like they'd discussed.

When all were seated, Josh folded his hands in front of him on the tabletop. All the boys quietly did the same.

He noticed Melissa's little smile as she also folded her hands in front of her, so Josh lowered his head before she noticed that he was smiling too. "Dear Heavenly Father, thank You for this good day and that we are joined as a family to share it together. Thank You for our guest and thank You for all this great food that we now get to eat. Amen."

"Amen!" they all shouted, except for Ryan, who shouted "Yea!"

Ryan slapped his hands over his mouth, then glanced sheepishly at Melissa. "I meant 'amen,' like Uncle Josh said."

She smiled back. "That's okay, Ryan. God likes everyone to be happy."

He nodded as he reached for the bowl of carrots. "I forgot what to say. Yesterday was the first time we did this."

Bradley nodded beside him. "Yeah. Uncle Josh says it's good for us. Like vegabulls. And God likes it too. We gotta start being spectfull to God. Like, cuz He made us and everything."

Josh pasted a smile on his face as he turned to Melissa. "It's a start."

Her returning smile made his heart do funny things. "It looks like you're doing wonderful, Uncle Josh. Pretty soon I'll have to give you my Sunday school teacher's job."

"Uh, I don't think so."

"I still can't believe I'm having turkey dinner on a Friday night. You even made stuffing."

"Don't be too impressed. It's the kind that comes out of a box."

"It still tastes good."

Andrew nodded. "Yeah. Uncle Josh makes lots of stuff that comes out of a box. He doesn't cook like Mom, but he makes lots of good stuff."

Kyle picked up the bowl of salad and handed it to Melissa. "I helped make the salad. Uncle Josh told me to."

"The salad looks delicious, Kyle. The whole meal is delicious."

Tyler rested his elbows on the table and grinned. "You should see the dessert, Miss Klassen. Uncle Josh finished it last night after the other kids were in bed. And then we hid it."

Bradley offered Melissa the bottle of salad dressing. "While

Uncle Josh got to do the fun stuff, we had to clean up. Are you pressed?"

"Pressed?" Melissa turned to Josh.

If he thought his cheeks were warm before, not only were they hot now, but so were his ears. "I, uh, told them I wanted you to be IMpressed by how neat the house was. I should have known better than to expect them to not say anything." He didn't think she was that impressed now, but if she would have seen the mad scramble to get everything picked up and the place vacuumed, she would have been. The place looked so different than a short hour before she got there that even he had been impressed.

"It's okay, Josh. I honestly don't know how you do it. I don't know if I could do it, and I have experience with children every day. Running a household is different than a classroom. I admit that at school I see them at their best. You have to dress them and feed them and get them there."

Ryan rested his hand on Melissa's arm to get her attention. "It's not so hard. Uncle Josh is happy if everyone has a lunch to take to school, no one goes to school naked, and no one goes to bed at night hungry."

"Ryan!" Tyler called out. "I don't think Miss Klassen wants to hear that."

Josh wanted to either bury his face in his hands or crawl under the table and never come out.

Ryan turned to Tyler. "But it's true! Uncle Josh says that all the time! I only sometimes have to pull old socks out of my hamper. I've never had to wear bare feet in my shoes."

Bradley started tugging on Melissa's sleeve. "Uncle Josh is doing a real good job looking after us. He really is."

"Yes, I know he is." For a split second, Melissa made eye contact with Josh, smiled, then let her gaze sweep over all five of the boys. "How would everyone like to tell me what you did at school today?"

He listened to the boys chatter on about school for the duration of their meal, grateful beyond words for Melissa being able to change the subject gracefully. All sound ceased when he returned with the chocolate cake, which he'd hidden on the top shelf of the cupboard above the fridge. He wondered if they heard the shuffle of him moving things from atop the fridge, which would necessitate him finding a different secret hiding spot for next time.

He placed the cake in the middle of the table as all five boys stared at it, each one no doubt hoping for the first piece. This time he thought it best to tell Melissa his secrets concerning the cake, before the boys blurted it out and embarrassed him any more. "This came out of a box too. It's a mix. It even had an envelope of icing in it. I figure if I do it carefully, I can get nine pieces out of it, and there's only seven of us, so that means the adults," he enunciated the word slowly, "can have two pieces."

"Aww! Uncle Josh! No fair!" a chorus of voices called out.

"I promised them I'd make a chocolate cake if they all behaved and did a good job cleaning the house before you got here. Do they deserve it, Miss Klassen? Or do we get the whole thing?"

Silence loomed as ten big round eyes zoomed in on Melissa. He gave her credit for letting the silence hang for as long as she did, to add to their suspense.

"I think they deserve it."

"Yea! I get first piece!"

"I get second!"

"Settle down. Everyone gets their piece when I give it to them—*after* they put their plates in the dishwasher."

In the blink of an eye, only Josh and Melissa remained in the dining room, the clatter and mad scramble in the kitchen echoing in the background as they jostled for position at the dishwasher.

Josh grinned from ear to ear. "That's a trick I learned from Brian and Sasha."

She grinned back. "It works."

"I'm first! I'm first!" Kyle ran into the dining room waving his arms over his head. He scuffled into his chair, the whole time watching Josh expectantly as his brothers rushed in behind him.

Josh began cutting the cake. "Do you think this is a good time to tell them the first shall be last, and the last shall be first?"

Melissa giggled, and Josh thought it a charming sound. "I don't think so."

Josh thought the cake was pretty good for a mix, especially since it was something he'd never done before. The whole thing had even come with a disposable pan to bake it in, making it quite easy to do, since there was nothing he had to figure out for himself. On the bad side, he had a feeling that after making one cake, he would be obligated to make more, since now they knew he could do it.

As expected, the second the kids finished their cake, they deserted the dining room and ran for the living room to play video games or to the den to fight for the computer, leaving Josh alone with Melissa.

"I want to help with the dishes."

He opened his mouth to protest, but before he could say a thing, she raised her palms to him and stood. "Don't argue with me. I think you're doing such a good thing by looking after the boys, and I'm sure you could use a break. You still had to make the meal, and I can't imagine what it took to get the house tidy for me on short notice, so let me help."

"You're not giving me a choice, are you?"

"Nope."

He had every intention of not doing the dishes until she left, then getting a couple of the kids to help by telling them that if they helped, they could stay up later, since it was a Friday night. In a strange kind of way, this was better. If he took Melissa into the living room, the boys would vie for her attention and yak her ear off. If they were in the kitchen doing the dishes, the boys would stay as far away as possible in fear of being asked to work.

This way he would have her all to himself, and he didn't have to share.

"How about if you wash and I dry, since I know where everything goes?"

"Sounds good to me. Let's get started now. I would think there's an awful lot to do."

"That's a matter of perspective, I guess. It's no different than any other day for me."

She followed him into the kitchen, and unlike the other times he met with Melissa in person, today they had no time constraints and nothing specific to discuss. The time flew by as they talked about nothing in particular, and for the first time, Josh thought that doing dishes wasn't so bad.

After he slid the last clean bowl into the cupboard, he leaned over to push the buttons to start the dishwasher. "What time should I pick you up tomorrow?"

Instead of Melissa's voice, Bradley's little voice replied, "Pick her up? Are you and Miss Klassen going out to a restaurant for supper tomorrow, Uncle Josh?"

Josh fumbled with the dish towel and turned around. "No, Bradley. We're going shopping—to the Christian bookstore. Miss Klassen and I are going to buy everyone their very own Bibles to read. You'll be allowed to read it before bed for credit on your reading minutes for school."

"But I can't read good yet."

"It's okay. I know that. I can read to you until you get better."

Bradley turned to Melissa. "You mean you're not going to a restaurant with my uncle Josh?"

"No, Bradley, we're not."

"But why not? Don't you like each other?"

Josh couldn't allow Bradley to put Melissa on the spot. More than that, he was afraid to know the answer. All he knew was how he felt, and he did like Melissa, at least for as little as he knew her. Through the eyes of a child, all Bradley could fathom in a relationship was "liking" someone, but in this case, the obstacles went too deep for Bradley to understand why dating Melissa wasn't a possibility. "Bradley, please. You're not supposed to ask questions like that. Why don't you go play video games with Ryan?"

Melissa turned to him. "It's okay, Uncle Josh," she said, then approached Bradley. She lowered herself by bending one knee and kneeling on the other to make herself eye level with the boy. "Of course I like your uncle. I think in time we could become good friends. Is that what you wanted to know?"

Bradley squinted his eyes, scrunched his eyebrows, and looked first at Melissa, then back to Josh. "But friends can still go to a restaurant for supper, right?"

Melissa nodded. "I suppose so, Bradley."

"So does that mean you're going to go for supper with Uncle Josh tomorrow?"

"Well. . ."

Josh forced himself to smile, something he seemed to be doing a lot of lately. "I don't know if Miss Klassen wants to go to a restaurant with me tomorrow, Bradley."

Bradley stepped closer to Melissa, who was still hunkered down in front of him. "You want to go with Uncle Josh tomorrow, don't you?"

"Uh. Sure I do, Bradley, but I don't know if Uncle Josh does."

"Uncle Josh?"

"Uh. Sure, Bradley, if Miss Klassen wants to go out for supper to a restaurant, we can do that—but only if she wants to."

"Yea!" Bradley shouted. "I'll go ask Tyler if he can baby-sit us!"

In a flash, Bradley disappeared.

Josh cleared his throat as Melissa stood. "Well, I guess we're going out for supper tomorrow. What time should I pick you up?"

"But we're going shopping tomorrow, aren't we?"

"How about if we go shopping later in the day, then go for an early supper?"

They both glanced toward the doorway to the living room,

where they both could hear Bradley's animated voice chattering away to his brothers about their plans for Saturday, then back to each other.

"I guess," she mumbled.

Josh cleared his throat. "Well, Melissa, it looks like we have ourselves a date."

eight

Josh tucked the bag of books under the seat and slid behind the wheel. "I can't believe how much that cost. I had no idea kids' books were that expensive."

"I know what you mean, especially when you had to buy five of them. But it's a real good start, and when the younger kids improve their reading skills, you can pass the books down from the older ones. There's what, two years between their ages all the way down the line?"

"Something like that. So, where do you want to go for supper?"

"I don't care, but I would think you don't want to go somewhere that serves hamburgers."

"You got that right. Steak?"

"Sure."

Josh started the van and drove out of the parking lot, heading for a steak house he'd driven by countless times yet never been to.

As he pulled into the parking lot, he scanned the row of parked cars, gladly noting he wasn't the only van in the bunch. To make himself feel better, he pulled into an empty spot beside another van.

He should have been driving his two-seater sports car to take a woman out for a Saturday evening dinner, not a family minivan, which he noticed the hard way was piled with toys and old hamburger wrappers and drink cans in the backseats. But being the practical type, he'd put his car into storage, since every time he traveled, he had a load of kids with him. At the price of car insurance, it didn't make sense to have the car sit in the garage, untouched, except for when the kids hit it when they put their bikes away.

Since they were earlier than the usual dinner crowd, they were shown straight to a table. Immediately, Josh knew they'd come to the right place. There wasn't a kid anywhere.

Neither of them spoke when they were seated. After a silence that was much too long for comfort, Josh folded his hands on the table and tried to act casual. "Well, here we are."

Melissa did the same. "Yes. I guess we are."

Silence hung between them, and for the life of him, Josh couldn't figure out what to say. They were supposed to be on a date, but because the only reason they were together was to satisfy a little kid, it felt like anything but a date.

If he had been with Theresa, he knew exactly what he would be doing. They would have started the night out by telling each other about what they'd done since the last time they'd been together, and Theresa would catch him up on the news of the week, which would have revolved around either a familiar activity or mutual friends. Then Theresa would have teased him about something dumb he'd done recently, and together they would share a good laugh.

But those days were gone. He wasn't here with Theresa, and this wasn't a real date. He was here with his nephew's teacher, a woman who had sacrificed time from her weekend to help him buy some books for the kids. He wasn't even sure she had wanted to go out to dinner with him. The only reason they were together was that Bradley put them in an awkward spot.

He suspected the main reason she went along with Bradley's prompting was because knowing Bradley's family situation, despite Josh's good intentions, it was obvious he didn't know what he was doing. In the best interest of one of her young students, she'd become involved in a situation that had quickly escalated out of control.

Josh ran his fingers through his hair. "I've got to be honest with you. I have no idea what to do or say. I've never been in a situation like this in my life."

Melissa stared down at her napkin. "I know. I don't know

what to do or say, either."

Fortunately, the waitress took that moment to appear, sparing Josh having to think of a reply.

Instead of concentrating on each other, they both studied the menus and exchanged only a few words on the possible selections.

Silence again hung in the air after the waitress took their orders and left them alone once more.

A different waitress walked past their table with orders for other patrons.

Josh leaned back in his chair and folded his hands to rest on his stomach. "Look, Melissa, broccoli. I do hope you're going to eat all your 'vegabulls.' "

She smiled, and Josh felt more encouraged about the way the evening might turn out. "You, Uncle Josh, are a tyrant."

"Yeah, but I'm a healthy tyrant."

"A healthy tyrant who hides chocolate cake. How could you?"

"Hey. If I didn't hide it, you wouldn't have had any. I made it after most of them went to bed for a good reason. I have no idea what I'm going to do at Christmastime when I have to hide their presents. I've been considering renting a storage locker, just to be safe." He closed one eye and raised one finger to his lips. "Hmm. . . Actually, I already have a storage locker. I'll just use that."

"I guess you put all your furniture into storage for as long as you're living at your brother's house."

"No, I didn't have that much stuff. My junk is in the basement. Except for my stereo and my TV, which are in my bedroom. What's in storage is my car. Between the van and the kids' bikes, there wasn't room in the garage for it. I guess I'll drive it again someday."

"This has been a big adjustment for you, hasn't it?"

Josh let go a very humorless laugh. "You have no idea."

She listened intently, laughing at times, as he told her about some of his experiences and mishaps in his first month of being Mr. Substitute Parent. They groaned together predicting some things that were bound to happen, as well as other potential disasters Josh saw coming but for now could do nothing about except let things develop naturally. After laughing so much, when the waitress brought their meals, they needed time to be silent and wind down to properly give thanks for the food and their day together.

Josh closed his eyes to savor his first bite of the delicious steak. "This is sooo good. And I don't have to share. Plus I can stay seated the whole time I eat."

He opened his eyes to see Melissa studying him. She didn't say a word.

He quickly dabbed at his mouth with his napkin. "Oops. Sorry. I didn't mean to sound like that. And I didn't mean to talk so much about the kids earlier. I thought it was only parents who went out to get away from the kids and then ended up talking about nothing else. I must be pretty pathetic."

"No, you're certainly not pathetic."

"Really?" he asked, not caring about the sarcastic edge to his voice. "If it wasn't for Bradley pulling that little stunt and backing both of us into a corner we wouldn't be here together right now. A six year old had to get me a date."

"It's okay, Josh. I'm having a good time."

He smiled from the bottom of his heart. "Me too. Still, I promise not to talk any more about the kids."

"I don't mind. What you're having to face is very unusual, especially at your age."

Josh smoothed his hair, then toyed with some of the food on his plate as he spoke. He knew lots of people his age who were married and had kids. "Not really. Lots of twenty-five year olds are parents."

"Yes, but most twenty-five-year-old fathers only have babies and toddlers, not a host of boys from fifteen years old all the way down to six."

"No, I suppose not. Up until a month ago, it was just me and Cleo."

"Yes, you've said that before. Cleo seems like a very nice dog."

"She's great. Have you ever had a dog? Bradley told me you've been asking a lot of questions about her. I've got a book on Labs if you're interested. It's full of general characteristics and expectations for the breed, training tips, plus all sorts of stuff you should know before you get any dog."

"That's okay. It's just that the whole situation, uh, interested me. That's all."

"If you ever want to borrow the book, just let me know. Although it's packed in a box somewhere—it might take me awhile to find it."

"I'll be sure to ask you for it when the day comes that I decide to get a dog."

The waitress delivered the bill signifying the end of their evening together. Josh snatched it up when he thought Melissa would get to it first. "This is my treat. It was supposed to be a date, you know, so that means I pay."

"Not really. Not anymore."

"It is for a first date." He didn't say it out loud, but besides being their first date, this would also be their last. The thought somehow caused considerable regret. "Do you think Bradley will be happy now? I told you he had a crush on you. He wouldn't have done this if he didn't think you should be treated special. You should hear all the things he tells me about you."

She cringed. "I don't think I want to know."

One corner of Josh's mouth quirked up. "Don't worry. It's all good." He folded his hands on the table after he gave the waitress his credit card. "Want a list?"

He could see her cheeks darken, even in the low restaurant lighting, and he tried not to smile because of it.

"No, I certainly do not want a list. Two can play at this game. He's always singing your praises too." Melissa stopped talking as the waitress returned with the slip for Josh to sign. "I'm pleased to announce that every good thing he says about you is true."

"Then what about the bad stuff? Is that true too?"

Her eyes sparkled as she smiled, then followed his lead as he stood. "He hasn't said anything bad. He has quite a case of hero worship for his resident uncle."

"I could say the same about his teacher."

Josh drove her home and walked her to the door with mixed feelings. Tonight was supposed to be a first date, in which case he would simply say a quick good night at the door. On the other hand, they'd been out together a number of times, although not a single instance could be called a date. In such a case, he knew her well enough to kiss her good night, which was exactly what he wanted to do. It was also exactly why he shouldn't. Not only was he not in a position to pursue a relationship, he could only guess at how awkward it would be for a teacher to see the parent or guardian of a student socially, and he was already pushing the boundaries.

She waved as she closed the door. "If they're still awake, say good night to Bradley for me. Good night, Josh, and thank you for a lovely evening. I hope I'll see you and the boys at church in the morning."

Before he could think about it any more, the door closed, so he went home.

&

"Miss Klassen! Miss Klassen!"

Melissa turned around to see the McMillian clan arriving through the main door with Bradley running ahead, waving his new book of Bible stories over his head.

She bent down as he reached her. "Good morning, Bradley. It's nice to see you at church again this morning."

"Look what Uncle Josh gave me!"

"It's very nice. Did you read any of it yet?"

He nodded so fast his hair bounced. "Yes! Some! But Uncle Josh helped lots."

Melissa straightened as the rest of the crowd, everyone carrying their own brand-new Bibles, joined them.

"It's good to see you again, Uncle Josh."

"It's good to see you, too, Miss Klassen. Would you care to join us?"

Joining him probably wasn't a good idea, but she told herself that since she would soon be leaving for her Sunday school class midway through the service, it would be okay to sit with him.

Being beside him as they sang the worship songs together felt different today than the week before. This time she had the comforting sensation of sitting beside a friend, rather than a mere acquaintance. When the time came to leave the sanctuary to take the children down to the Sunday school classrooms, for the first time in her life, she experienced some hesitation at leaving to do something she loved.

Just like the previous week, Bradley still remained after the other children left, helping her pick up the materials and tidy the room until his entire family stormed in the door.

Bradley dropped the books he had been so neatly stacking and called from across the room. "Uncle Josh! Are we going to the restaurant for lunch again? Are we? Please?"

"I don't know, Bradley. We went out last week, and we can't do that too often."

"But what if Miss Klassen can come? Can we go out then?"

Melissa hadn't seen the bill for last week, but she could only guess how much it cost to feed seven people at a restaurant. "It's okay, Bradley. We don't need to go to a restaurant two weeks in a row."

His eyes widened, and his smile stretched from ear to ear. "You mean you're coming to our house for lunch instead of going out? Wow!" He turned to Josh before Melissa could correct him. "Uncle Josh! Miss Klassen said she can come to our house for lunch!"

"Uh. . .I don't think that's what she said, Bradley." Josh turned to her, and the room hushed with a very pregnant pause as all the kids glued every micron of their attention to him, waiting for him to continue. "Although if she wants to come to our house for lunch, she's more than welcome—if she doesn't mind the mess. . . ."

Melissa tried not to let her smile show. She could remember as a child the occasional mad rush out the door on the Sunday mornings when they were running behind schedule. Knowing Josh and the boys had not yet established a Sunday morning routine, she could only guess at the things that happened in the process to make it out the door on time.

She looked down at Bradley, fully intending to let Josh save face by turning Bradley down so as not to witness their messy house, but Bradley's expectant expression stopped her words before they left her mouth.

She didn't know why Bradley wanted to see so much of her, but she suspected it had something to do with the ordeal of his parents moving away and knowing it could be years before he saw them again. Her heart broke for him at his lack of a tangible mother figure in his life, especially now knowing that Cleo was just a dog.

"That's okay, Uncle Josh. I'd love to come over to your house for lunch. I promise to not look at the mess." She bent down to whisper to Bradley but whispered loudly enough for all the boys and Josh to hear. "I didn't make my bed this morning, either."

Giggling sounded behind her, and Josh's cheeks turned a charming shade of pink, something she was discovering happened a lot, which added to his appeal. She stood and looked up to Josh for his final decision.

"That's great. It's nice that you can come. It looks like you've got everything put away, so we can all go. Do you remember how to get there?"

"Of course, but I'll follow you anyway."

Approximately every fifteen seconds of the trip behind the McMillian family van, the three youngest boys who were sitting in a row in the backseat turned around to wave at her. Sometimes she smiled and waved back. A few times all three of them turned to wave at the same time, then all abruptly turned around and sat still facing the front simultaneously, but it never lasted long.

For the first time, she appreciated her nice, silent car where the only sound was the purr of the engine or the music, only when she chose to turn it on, at the volume she personally selected.

On their arrival, this time Josh held Cleo with all four paws firmly on the ground while she patted and greeted the dog. The second Josh released Cleo, she jumped on every one of the boys, then Josh, to individually greet them all.

"Does she do this every time you come home?"

"Yup. Come on in. Just kick your way through the toys and have a seat on the couch. I'll get lunch together."

"Forget it, Uncle Josh. I'm helping."

As she followed Josh into the kitchen, she glanced quickly back over her shoulder to see Bradley, his face shining with glee. Immediately, she knew she had made the right decision to accompany them for lunch.

"You don't have to set the dining room table for lunch. I don't mind staying in the kitchen. It's cozy."

"I would never have called seven people squashed around a table 'cozy,' but it is easier to keep everyone in here to eat."

"Then it's settled. Let me do something."

Josh removed two egg cartons and a jug of milk from the fridge, then pulled a huge frying pan from the cupboard. "Here. You can make the scrambled eggs, I'll make the toast and set the table."

She looked down at the egg cartons without touching them. "I have no idea how much to make."

"I figure we can get away with fourteen eggs."

"Fourteen eggs!"

Josh closed one eye and started counting on his fingers. "Maybe you're right. Use fifteen. If there's any left, we can give it to Cleo. She loves eggs."

"You're going to toast the whole loaf of bread, aren't you?"

"Probably." He grinned. "If you think this is bad, you should see how much ketchup we go through in a week."

Melissa shook her head as she started cracking the eggs. "I don't know how you do it."

"It's easy. I figure how much I would eat when I was living by myself, and then quadruple it. I'm usually close."

They worked together to prepare lunch with a friendly camaraderie. When Josh called for the boys to come to the table, they all jostled into place around the kitchen nook, which Melissa could only compare to a restaurant booth, except larger.

Again she somehow found herself sitting beside Josh, but accredited it to the fact that since now the same number of bodies surrounded the table as what they considered normal, she and Josh had taken the accustomed places of the boys' parents, which were probably side by side.

When Josh spoke, all the boys quieted. "Who wants to say grace? Okay, Bradley."

"Dear God. Thanks for lunch. And thanks for my fambley. And thanks for Cleo, who is a great dog. And thanks that Miss Klassen could come too. Amen."

Melissa barely had time to mumble her answering "amen" when a multitude of hands reached at once for the mountain of toast in the middle of the table. As the scrambled eggs were eagerly devoured, they talked about their morning in church and how all their classes went. Andrew gave her a summary of the sermon, then Tyler asked if he could bring his friend Allyson next Sunday morning, to which Josh readily agreed.

Once the food was gone, as quickly as they had come, they deserted the kitchen leaving Melissa alone with Josh once more.

"It's like this every day, isn't it?"

He shrugged his shoulders as he dumped exactly two spoon-fuls of leftover eggs into Cleo's bowl, along with a piece of half-eaten toast. "More or less."

Cleo gobbled up the contents of her bowl, giving Melissa more insight as to how Cleo had gotten so fat.

"Don't you think that—"

A thump followed by a screech sounded from the living room. "Uncle Josh! Uncle Josh! Kyle turned off my game!"

"Ryan hit me!"

"You made me lose my man!"

"Ow! Ow!"

"Excuse me," Josh mumbled over his shoulder as he ran into the living room. She could hear his stern voice scolding them as he broke up the fight, followed by orders to both of them to apologize.

Melissa sank to the table, unable to stop herself from listening.

Josh McMillian was a very special man to take on such responsibility and to handle everything so well. Without a doubt, he would have his frustrations, and from being a teacher experienced with young children, she knew at times he would blow it, as everyone did. She could also see that when that happened, he would apologize to the boys the same as he made them apologize to each other, then move on, and all would be well again.

Melissa sighed. When the time came for Josh to leave his nephews with their parents, he would make a wonderful parent to children of his own. Going hand in hand with that, she also knew without a doubt he would be a wonderful husband and partner to the right woman.

She suddenly found herself jealous of a woman whom she had never met.

She had established herself as wrong in her foolish assumption about Cleo, and she hoped and prayed she would never have to reveal her secret.

Because she had thought Cleo was human, Melissa had made the suggestion that Josh see a couples counselor. At the time, Josh hadn't known she had been referring to Cleo. Instead of questioning why she would suggest such a thing, Josh replied that he had decided he wouldn't marry the woman he thought she was referring to. Therefore, even though it wasn't Cleo, there was in fact a woman with whom

Josh had some form of serious relationship. For the time being, he had decided against marriage with this woman, but that didn't mean the situation wouldn't change or that it was beyond hope. Josh's life was in a state of upheaval, and a million things could and would change in the next few months, to say nothing of the possible extent of time he would be caring for his nephews.

Whatever the state of his present relationship, it only magnified the mandate of her principal. For now, Josh did not consider marriage an option. That didn't say he wasn't still going out with her, nor did it mean things would not change. Just because Bradley had set them up for a date didn't negate the fact that in her mind, it was still a date. And being a date, she had stepped between Josh and someone else, and that was a recipe for disaster.

Professionally, it could mean her job and her reputation.

Personally, to continue on and hope that something would change beyond her true relationship with Josh, which was only as the legal guardian of one of her students, was an invitation to heartbreak, frustration, and unrealistic expectations. More so, it was a breach of trust, to say nothing of dishonorable, to come between a man and a woman in an existing relationship, even if that relationship was experiencing some difficulties. Josh's whole life was in a state of flux. He needed help, not a catalyst to weaken his situation or cause him more stress.

Most of all, Josh McMillian needed a friend. A good Christian friend who could offer him a shoulder to lean on when he was weak, and someone who could help him when his load became too heavy.

Before she could formulate a way to do that, Josh reappeared.

"Sorry about that. I think they're going to be okay—at least for a few minutes."

Melissa stood. "I think I'd better be going, before Bradley decides that it's so late that I might be staying for supper, too. I don't want to intrude on your hospitality."

"Don't worry, you could never do that."

"Still, I think it's time I went home. But please, if there's anything I can ever do for you, please, let me know."

To Melissa's surprise, instead of walking her to the door, Josh stepped in front of her and picked up both her hands in his. Shivers ran up her spine as he rubbed his callused thumbs over the tender skin of her wrists. "You've already done so much for me. I don't know how I'll ever be able to thank you."

She struggled to find her voice. "Everything I've done, I've done for Bradley. I meant it when I said that if there's anything you need help with, you can call me. Anything. Name it."

"Well, actually there is."

Her heart quickened. Standing like this, with her hands nestled inside his larger ones, he was so close he could kiss her.

"When Bradley gets to school first thing in the morning, could you make sure the lid to his thermos is tight?"

nine

"McMillian! Telephone for you!"

Josh wiped his hands on his rag and shoved the cloth into the pocket of his coveralls. "Coming!" he called, and hurried to the phone with his heart in his throat. None of his friends ever called him at work, and if the caller was a customer Rick would have taken it. After all the interruptions and extra time off he'd taken, he'd instructed the kids not to call unless someone had been hurt or it was some other form of emergency.

He didn't know if he could handle another trip to the hospital. God had provided a miracle to save Bradley from things he didn't want to think about the first time. Josh wasn't so sure that the next time something happened to one of the kids, the outcome would be so minimal.

A phone call half an hour after the close of school did not bode well.

By the time he reached the phone, his heart was pounding. "Hello?" he choked out, hoping unreasonably that it was only a charity soliciting for donations.

"Uncle Josh?" a little kid voice questioned.

Josh thought he might faint. "Bradley. What's wrong?"

"Uncle Josh, there's something wrong with Miss Klassen's car. I know there wasn't really anything wrong with it last time, but this time there is. For really. I heard her say that yesterday the car nearly never started and she wasn't sure it would even go. You gotta do something!"

Josh bowed his head, squeezed his eyes shut, and pinched the bridge of his nose with his thumb and index finger. "Bradley, I thought I told you not to call me at work unless it was an emergency."

"But it is a mergencie. Miss Klassen needs her car. What if

it won't work in the morning, and she can't come to school?"

Josh sighed. If her car didn't start, she would simply take a cab or call someone else to pick her up, since she lived so close to the school. However, the greater worry was that her car would die en route somewhere, leaving her stranded and at the mercy of any whacko who wanted to prey on a single, defenseless woman. He stopped himself from such thinking. He didn't want to consider such a thing. It had been less than a week since he'd last asked about her car, and it had been fine then.

"I doubt it's that bad, Bradley, or she would have called me herself."

"But Tyler said he can make hot dogs for supper so you can go to Miss Klassen's house and fix her car. And then you and Miss Klassen can have pizza at her house for supper. You know, while you're fixing her car."

He almost told Bradley he knew Melissa's car was perfectly fine, but then the thought crossed his mind that Bradley was genuinely worried if he had gone so far as convince Tyler to do any work, especially to cook for the whole family.

Josh knotted his brows and looked up at the clock. He was off in an hour. If Tyler fed the rest of them, he could conceivably have a look at Melissa's car and even do a minor repair, and still make it back home in plenty of time to help the kids with their homework and get the younger ones to bed on time for a school night.

"Are you at home or at Darlene's?"

"I'm at home."

"What about everyone else?"

"Everyone is at home, and we're all doing our homework."

Josh opened his mouth, but no words came out. If everyone was doing their homework without prompting or threats, he was going to leave well enough alone.

He cleared his throat. "Okay, tell Tyler to make hot dogs, and I'll be home as soon as I can figure out what's wrong with Miss Klassen's car."

"Yippee! Uh, I mean, that's good, Uncle Josh. I hope you can fix it okay."

"I'm sure I can. See you later, Sport."

❧

"What do you mean, you're here to fix my car? There's nothing wrong with my car."

Josh let go a long, tired sigh and squeezed his eyes shut for a second. "Bradley said that you said it barely started yesterday for you. Why didn't you call me?"

Melissa bowed her head and dragged her palm down her face. "It was only the battery. I left the headlights on when I went in to do some grocery shopping. I drove it for awhile after that, and the battery is all charged up and working just fine now. So really and truly, there is nothing wrong with my car. I don't know how Bradley heard me say that, because I was talking to one of the other teachers about my little misadventure while we were standing in the parking lot. I also said at the same time that it's fully recharged. I don't understand why Bradley is doing this. You said before you think he has a crush on me and he wants to do something special for me, but I don't think that's it."

"No, I thought so at first, but I changed my mind. If he had a crush on you, he'd want to spend every minute he could with you. He made no attempts to come with me. In fact, he was pretty happy when I told him I was going directly to your house after work, obviously alone. I wonder if he and the boys are trying to get rid of me? Not only is Tyler making supper, but Bradley said that at 3:30 they were all doing their homework without me asking first, when I wasn't even there."

"This sounds serious. What do you think we should do?"

"If there really isn't anything wrong with your car, I think I should go straight home and see what they're all really doing."

"Maybe I should come with you."

Josh glanced to the street, to the parked van. He wouldn't make any points for stealth driving the lumbering vehicle. His only advantage would be that the kids wouldn't be expecting him home for at least another hour, so he had the element of time on his side.

While he was still contemplating the possibilities, Melissa's voice interrupted his mental meanderings, trying to figure out what they were really doing.

"How about if we took my car? Then they wouldn't see you coming."

Josh grinned. "Good thinking."

"I'm a teacher. One day I'll tell you about some of the ways I find out what the kids don't want me to know."

He pretended to shudder. "Maybe I had better be careful what I say around you too."

Melissa winked. "You'd be surprised what I already know about you."

"If it's stuff Bradley's been saying, I don't think I want to know."

She laughed but didn't comment as she disappeared inside to fetch her purse, then locked up.

Josh felt strange being a passenger while a woman drove. He'd never been a passenger when he and Theresa went out, but then they had always been in his car, and it had been natural for him to drive.

"Have you caught them doing anything sneaky lately? Hiding things? Is your birthday coming up?"

He leaned back in the seat and raised his arms, linking his fingers behind his head. "Is that your subtle way of getting more information out of me?"

"I'm trying to think of why the kids would want you out of the house. If it is your birthday coming up, then I'm going to turn around right now and not ruin their surprise."

"My birthday isn't for over six months. It's not that. It's also too early to do Christmas shopping, and even if it wasn't too early, I doubt they'd be that discreet. It's got to be something else."

"What about the computer? Could they be doing something

they don't want you to see?"

"No. I installed a filtering program. It freezes the computer and shuts down the application if they're getting into something I don't want them into. I also have a monitoring program where I can see what they've been looking at on-line, and I check it every few days. It's not that."

"Could they be covering up for one of the older boys? Maybe Tyler and his girlfriend?"

"Trust me. As close as the boys are, there would have to be some pretty high bribery involved for them to participate in hiding something for Tyler. They get their greatest joys from tattling on each other. I can't say I mind." He turned to her and grinned widely, but Melissa kept her attention intently focused on the rush-hour traffic.

The second Melissa stopped in front of the house, they ran out of the car and straight for the front door, which Josh found wasn't locked.

He sniffed deeply, but didn't smell burning cigarettes or anything worse that he didn't want to think about, even though he had to be realistic. No music blared, and all was quiet, not even the voices of quiet conversation.

Josh strode into the living room to find Andrew half sitting and half lying on the couch with a book in his lap. He raised his eyes only briefly, then continued to read. "Hey, Uncle Josh. That was quick," he mumbled.

Josh ran into the den, where Tyler was on the computer, alone, an encyclopedia program open to a South American country Josh knew Tyler was studying for his geography class. "Hi, Uncle Josh. What are you doing here? There was one hot dog left, but I gave it to Cleo."

His stomach sank. The dog hadn't greeted them at the door. "Where's Cleo?"

"Bradley and Ryan took her next door. Mr. Wright's son wants to get a Lab, so he asked if someone could take Cleo over for a few minutes to meet him. I hope you don't mind."

Melissa appeared in the doorway. "Kyle is almost finished

with his math homework. I don't know where Bradley and Ryan are."

Josh turned around and guided her out of the den and into the kitchen, which was a mess but, overall, wasn't extreme considering the boys made their own supper. "They're next door with Cleo. On a legitimate errand. I can't believe this. Something's not right—I just can't figure out what it is."

"Maybe everything is exactly as it appears to be. They made their own supper, they're doing their homework without being nagged, and everything is fine."

"Wow. . ." Josh let his voice trail off. "I feel really bad for dragging you over here like this for nothing. Not that I'm not glad it is nothing. I don't know what to think."

"I think we should go back to my house so you can get your van. How's that for a start?"

"Yeah, that's a good idea."

He returned to the den to tell Tyler that he was going out again, where Tyler grunted a response and continued on with his homework assignment. Andrew waved from the couch, barely lifting his eyes from the book.

Halfway to Melissa's house, Josh's stomach grumbled.

He rested both his open palms on his tummy. "Excuse me. I haven't had supper yet. Have you?"

"No, actually, I haven't. I'm glad your stomach started making noises before mine did."

"Bradley suggested we order pizza while I worked on your car that doesn't need fixing, so why don't we go somewhere for pizza? Apparently they made me a hot dog, but then Tyler gave it to the dog."

"I thought wieners were bad for dogs, that they were a choking hazard."

Josh nodded. "They are. I showed the kids how to slice it down the center first, before cutting it up for Cleo."

"You're kidding. No wonder that dog is so fat."

"But she's happy. And you haven't answered my question. Want to go out and grab a pizza?"

"I suppose so. I haven't eaten yet, either, and I don't have plans."

She pulled into the parking lot of the nearest strip mall containing a pizzeria. He'd ordered from them once but had never been inside.

Like most typical Italian restaurants, the lights were dim, and a candle in a yellow glass holder glowed from the center of each table, each covered with a red-and-white checkered cloth.

Josh thought it was perfect. In a place like this, they could talk and have a private conversation, yet it wasn't cozy or intimate enough to be the kind of place he would take a woman on a date.

He folded his hands on the tabletop. "I'm lost for ideas. What do you think they're up to?"

"I don't know. Tyler, Andrew, and Kyle didn't seem to care whether we were there or not."

"Bradley and Ryan were out with the dog, visiting the neighbor, who's known them since they were born. Alice is probably feeding them some kind of cake right now, and they'll be especially happy that they got something made with sugar, and their brothers didn't."

"You could think about this until the cows come home and still not come up with an answer, you know."

"I know. Kinda scary, isn't it?"

"That's parenthood, Josh. I think you're learning the hard way, but you've been blessed that they really are good kids."

"I know. I thank God for them every day."

"Have you heard from your brother recently? I'll bet they miss the boys, and I'm sure the boys miss their parents."

"I got a very short letter last week. It hasn't really been a long time since they've been gone, and they've got a lot of new things to settle into, so he said they won't be writing often. They'll have some computer time coming after awhile—the clinic is apparently strict with it, but eventually we'll be able to send E-mail back and forth. That will be good. The kids will like that. They do miss their parents, but for now, it has almost been a vacation for them having me around. It's starting to get into more of a routine. I can feel the difference in our relationship since I first moved in. I'm no longer a novelty, and I'm not always fun anymore."

"If you ever need to get away on short notice, I'm usually home. If you need someone to talk to with experience with kids, you can call me anytime, even in the middle of the night."

"That's very nice of you to offer. I might have to take you up on that someday. Or night."

He grinned, and Melissa grinned back.

Even though he would probably never know why Bradley had become so overly concerned with Melissa's car, he had to appreciate the opportunity to spend some unencumbered time with her. Knowing all was under control at home and he had nothing to worry about allowed him to enjoy himself fully. Unlike Saturday night, when their evening together was supposed to be a date, tonight came with no strings attached and no pressure.

The time flew by quickly, and before he knew it, he should have been home already, and they still hadn't made it back to Melissa's house to retrieve the van.

Melissa giggled as she stopped her car in the middle of the quiet residential street, allowing him to hop out of her car and directly into the van without having to see her to her own door. Strangely, he would have liked to have seen her to the door, even though there was nothing he was in a position to do once he got there.

By the time he arrived at home, all homework had been completed, the boys were back to playing computer and video games, and Tyler had the phone permanently affixed to his ear. Tyler's occasional grunts of agreement told Josh who Tyler was talking to.

Since the kitchen was clean, Josh flopped down on the couch, and Cleo hopped up beside him for a good scratch.

Josh smiled. For the first time since he moved in to pursue

his role as the boys' guardian, he felt at peace.

❧

"McMillian! Telephone for you!"

Josh wiped his hands on his rag at the same time as he jogged to the office to take the call. If Bradley was calling two days in a row to interrupt him at work for another wild-goose chase, for the first time he was going to have to dream up a punishment suitable for a six year old, an unpleasant chore Josh did not look forward to.

"Josh?"

"Melissa?" Josh's heart nearly stopped. In only saying his name, he detected a slight tremor in her voice. "What's wrong?"

"I don't know. Don't worry, it's not Bradley. I think there might be something wrong with my car."

"Might be?"

"Bradley told me that you talked to him this morning about the false alarms, and I told him how much I appreciated his concern, but something he said made me stop and think. He was genuinely worried about my car, and he seemed like he really thought there was something wrong with it. I'm probably worrying for nothing, but they found a knife hidden on the school grounds today, so the topic of vandalism and violence was the major point of discussion in the staff room at lunchtime. All the teachers are a little nervous right now, and a bulletin was sent out to the parents. You'll get it tonight. Anyway, this whole thing has made me stop and think. I wonder if Bradley saw something he can't quite put his finger on to describe. He is only six years old."

"I don't understand."

"I don't think any of the grade one kids are capable of hating me so badly to do something to my car, but this school has kids up to grade seven. Some of them would happily do something bad to a teacher's car, not for retribution but just for kicks. I'm not talking letting the air out of the tires, because that's happened once. I'm talking real damage. I'm wondering if it's possible one of the older kids has been touching my car. Maybe someone loosened something or tampered with it. What if Bradley saw one of the bigger kids hanging around my car and that's why he's so worried? He's sent you over here twice for what we thought was nothing. Maybe it's not nothing."

Josh could only guess at how difficult it had been to ask when she worried about overreacting. Still, she had to be prepared and know for sure. The thought that someone could have tampered with Melissa's car made his stomach churn. "You know I'll gladly come and have a look at it anytime, Melissa. They say the greatest fear is the fear of the unknown. Do you keep your car locked in the school parking lot?"

"Yes, but it wouldn't be hard or impossible for someone to squeeze in underneath, especially a child. The current enrollment is now nearly four hundred students, and that's a lot of kids to keep track of at once. Unfortunately, sometimes kids can be devious, especially the older ones, or sometimes they aren't able to draw the line between what seems like a fun prank and something that can turn into real danger."

"Where are you now? Did you drive it home?"

"Yes, I'm at home, but I was sweating the whole way. Do you think you could come by this evening sometime to have a look at it?"

"If I'm not sure what I'm looking for, or if it could be something as simple as something being loose, I prefer to check it out in daylight. Let me call home, and I'll probably be able to come right from work. I've got some money stashed in the house for emergency pizza—I'm sure the kids will be happy with that."

"You don't know how much I appreciate this, Josh."

"Not a problem. See you soon."

ten

Melissa could only see Josh from the waist down, encased in his usual blue coveralls, as he leaned far into the engine compartment of her car. She didn't know what he could hear with his head tucked way down there, especially over the noise as he tapped and banged on various parts of the engine, but she had to know.

She rested her hands on the fender and peeked down with no idea what to look for. "Have you found anything?"

His voice echoed strangely from his awkward position, but he didn't straighten. "Not so far. Can you shine that flashlight here for me?"

She tried her best to aim it on what she thought he was trying to see, then backed up quickly when he straightened.

"It doesn't look like anything's been touched, but I want to have a look from underneath, just to be sure. Wait for a sec. I brought my dolly from the shop."

Melissa waited while he walked to his van and removed what she could best describe as a surfboard with wheels. He put it on the ground beside her car, sat on it, and then leaned back on one elbow as he prepared to lie down on his back on the unit. "Can I have the flashlight?" he asked as he lowered himself fully, then stuck out his hand.

Melissa hesitated for only a second. Instead of giving it to him, she hid it behind her back. "May I have the flashlight?"

"What? Do you think you know where someone might have done something?"

"No, you're missing my point. You're talking to a teacher. I know you're perfectly capable of using the flashlight, but you're asking if you may have it."

Before she realized what he was doing, Josh was off the

112

dolly and stood no more than an inch in front of her. Laughter radiated from his eyes, and one side of his mouth quirked up. He lowered his head slightly to just the right spot. . .as if he was going to kiss her.

Melissa's chest constricted to a point she had to tell her body to inhale and exhale. She should have backed up, but her feet wouldn't move.

"Okay, Teacher. May I have the flashlight?"

Her heart nearly stopped when he reached behind her, keeping his body parallel with hers by lowering himself slightly and bending at the knees. He was so close, from head to toe, she could feel the warmth of his breath on her cheek in the cooling evening air when he reached behind her. Almost in slow motion, he gently removed the flashlight from her hand, still behind her back, then stepped back, very slowly.

The reprimand for not saying "please" wouldn't come out. All she could do was stare as he laid back down on the dolly and pushed himself underneath her car, so again all she could see was the lower half of him.

What was she doing? By not simply giving him the flashlight when he asked for it, she had goaded him into doing something she wasn't sure she could define. She didn't know why she did it, but she had dared him into taking action to obtain possession of the flashlight. What she hadn't expected was for him take her up on it in that way.

She had teased him, and her actions had backfired. Instead, he had teased her. He could have kissed her, right in the middle of her driveway, and she wouldn't have stopped him. If she had to be honest with herself, for that split second in time, she had wanted him to kiss her.

And that was wrong.

This was Josh McMillian. The guardian of one of her students. A man whose life was in such a dramatic state of transition she should have been helping him to get his life in order, not further complicating his life with hints of something neither of them were in any position to do anything about. The man was in some phase of a relationship with another woman. He had never spoken of her except to say he wouldn't marry her, but without knowing the background or being positive there was no chance of reconciliation, she still didn't consider him truly free.

She was doing exactly what she had promised herself she would not do when she didn't know Cleo was a dog, and that was to step in the middle of an existing relationship.

It was too late to think about Principal Swain's mandate about not getting involved with the parent of a student. The best she could do now would be to temper whatever was building into a controllable level, knowing it would be unrealistic to think she could go back to the impersonal parent and teacher association she maintained with her other students' families.

The scrape of the metal wheels of the dolly against the cement of the driveway snapped her mind back to where it should have been in the first place.

Josh stood, then began to unbutton the coveralls as he spoke. "You're fine. Every bolt and nut is tight, every line is intact, every wire and cable is untouched." He stepped out of the legs, and draped the garment over his arm, leaving him in rumpled jeans and a T-shirt. "I'm glad you called. I hope this puts your mind at ease. I'll be sure to tell Bradley when I get home that everything is fine and he won't have to worry any more about your car. I wish I could find out what it is that makes him have me check up on you so much."

"I wish I could figure it out too. While you're here, would you like to stay for supper? It's the least I can do."

"That would be great. The kids are ordering pizza, so there won't be anything left for me. You can bet that Cleo won't be getting anything, either."

"Since I've been standing outside, I don't have anything ready, and I forgot to take something out of the freezer. How about Tuna Noodle Casserole?"

He smiled, and Melissa almost forgot what she suggested.

"That sounds good. I haven't had that for a long time. The kids won't eat anything made out of fish or seafood of any kind. Can I help?"

"Oh, sure. You can open the can. I buy the kind of casserole that comes in a box. Add water, a can of tuna, simmer, and serve."

"I buy lots of stuff that starts out in a box. Bradley probably told you that already."

She chuckled as she led him into the house. "Actually, I think it was one of the other boys."

Josh sat at the kitchen table while Melissa removed the box from the cupboard.

"Tonight when you go home, I wonder if it would be a good idea to take Bradley aside and ask him what's bothering him. I don't really have time during the school day for that. Also, if he really does have a crush on me, I don't want to break his little heart. So far, he's done nothing in the class to indicate any special feelings toward me, which is another thing that doesn't add up. All he does is talk about you."

"I probably should be the one to ask him. Today is the first time you've called me, not Bradley, to come and see you, but really, it's from Bradley's prompting. Or maybe we should talk to him together. Tomorrow night is Boys Club and the youth group meeting, as well as that adult Bible study at Mike and Patty's house. How about if I pick you up, and we can take the kids out for an ice cream cone or something, and take Bradley aside and talk to him privately?"

"That sounds like a good idea." She placed the lid on the supper. "It's just got to simmer for twenty minutes. Want to watch television or something?"

Melissa flipped on the television to a popular sitcom, but neither of them paid much attention to the show. First Josh told her all about his day at work, mostly about how one of their best customers had paid an unbelievable amount of money on fixing up an older car for her grandson. She listened with fascination when he told her about his own first car, and then what directed his decision to become an auto mechanic as his livelihood.

Knowing she didn't know much, if anything, about cars, Josh tempered his descriptions to what she could understand, leaving out anything technical or what he didn't think she would be interested in, which she greatly appreciated. A few times she couldn't help herself and teased him because she knew a little about cars, just not much.

The timer went off to signify the casserole was ready.

Melissa stood. "I have a far better tool than you do. In case something goes wrong with my car, I have the world's greatest automotive tool. It's guaranteed to help me fix whatever is wrong, even in the middle of the night."

Instead of getting up, Josh leaned farther back on the couch and crossed his arms over his chest. "Really?"

"Yes. I have the world's greatest handyman's tool: my cell phone and the number to a great mechanic."

With that statement, Melissa sauntered into the kitchen with her nose in the air, and Josh following, laughing all the way.

She couldn't remember the last time she'd had a man over to her house for supper, if she ever had. Being at home instead of in a restaurant gave their time together less formality, and she liked it that way. When dinner was over and Josh had to leave, she felt strangely sad to see him go.

On the bright side, she knew she would see him again tomorrow.

Melissa closed the door when the van was no longer in sight and returned to the kitchen, humming.

ta

"Hello, Bradley. Are we ready to go?"

"Yes, Miss Klassen. We saved the front seat for you. Next to Uncle Josh."

Melissa smiled. "Thank you, Bradley. I'll be right there."

Bradley waited politely while she locked the house, and then he accompanied her to the van, opening the door for her. She wondered if he learned his good manners from his parents or from his uncle.

She noticed that Josh didn't attempt to talk the entire drive to the church. The boys all had something to say to her, except for Tyler who sat quietly in the back.

She accompanied Josh inside the building to see the boys to their individual groups, and then they continued on to the Flannigans' home in relative silence. Melissa didn't say a word, choosing to let Josh simply enjoy what she suspected was a rare quiet.

Since they had arrived separately last week, many eyebrows raised as people watched them arrive together this time. Melissa tried to suppress the nagging thought that sometime in the future Josh would eventually bring another woman, a woman with whom he would be pursuing a real relationship, not simply being with his youngest ward's teacher because they were trying to solve a problem.

The meeting went much the same as the previous week, except that this time, when the goodies were served, they left together.

As Josh pulled into traffic, he glanced quickly at her over his shoulder and voiced what she'd been thinking about most of the evening.

"I guess this is it. In a few minutes it'll be time to ask Bradley why he keeps sending me over to fix your car when there's nothing wrong with it. Plus I'm still not convinced that I didn't tighten his thermos good enough, even the first time, bringing me to the school three days in a row. I'm not sure it was completely because he wanted the fries, either. Bradley just isn't that devious."

Melissa nodded. "I know. He's so sweet in class. He's helpful to the other kids, and he always behaves well. I did notice a difference in his attention span when his parents moved away, but it seems to have gone back to normal recently. Are the other boys handling their parents being gone okay?"

"Within reason. I can tell when something unexpected reminds them of Brian and Sasha. Every so often, one of them will be really quiet for awhile, but they seem to get over it quickly enough. I don't know that I would have handled that kind of thing well as a kid. I think what's holding them together is that they are all positive it's only temporary, even though they've clearly been told it could be years."

"I still can't imagine looking after five kids who aren't my own on a long-term basis. I truthfully don't think I'd want to have five kids even of my own in this day and age. I doubt people ask you to your face, but I'd bet everyone you know is wondering why you're doing this."

He shrugged his shoulders and sighed. "As you can guess, this condition of Sasha's has been in existence for years, maybe even her whole life. Over the years, it's gotten worse and worse, and changing her medication hasn't been working anymore. One night, Brian was really down about it, and he started telling me about this clinic in Switzerland he'd been looking into. He said that with some extra medical insurance he'd picked up years ago before the problem became so extreme, plus some extra he'd been saving on the side, he could actually afford to take her. The only thing that was stopping them from trying it as a last resort was the kids."

"And that made you offer to take the kids and raise them on your own?"

"I've tried over the years to share the good news and the hope Jesus gives to all who believe, but when a person does nothing but talk, it's just hollow words. So I guess I put my money where my mouth is. Brian talked about how the boys needed to stay put in school, with their friends, in their own home, and to stay together. He could have put them in foster care, but no home would be able to take five of them at once, and even if they could have found someplace that would, it's not the same, having paid care instead of your own family. They're all the family I've got, I couldn't not do it. So I said I'd look after the kids until Sasha got well enough to come home and everything got back to normal."

Melissa turned to study Josh as they pulled into the church

parking lot. "Is that very likely?"

"No. But miracles do happen. I'm not going to count it out."

"We don't have time now, but next time we get together, would you like to pray for Sasha?"

His smile was the saddest she'd ever seen. It nearly brought tears to her eyes. "Yes. I'd like that. Thank you."

"I guess we should go get the kids, then."

"Yeah."

Once everyone was buckled into their seat belts, Josh announced that they were all going out for ice cream. The resounding cheer nearly made the van shake, showing Melissa that he hadn't told them of his plans beforehand.

Since they had to sit in two booths, Josh and Melissa easily sequestered Bradley with them, allowing the other four boys what they thought was more freedom, since they didn't have an adult at their table.

Josh casually licked his ice cream, then, resting one elbow on the table, leaned forward toward Bradley. "I've got to ask you something, Sport."

Bradley didn't eat his ice cream as delicately as his uncle. Bradley was already almost down to the cone, making Melissa want to poke Josh to get him to talk faster.

"I want to know why you've been sending me to fix Miss Klassen's car when there's nothing wrong with it."

Bradley's tongue stopped moving midlick, then started again much more slowly. "I thought there was something wrong. She even said so."

Melissa rested her elbows on the table, holding the cone in the air in front of her. "I didn't, Bradley. I told you it was something that happened to all cars, not just mine. And when you sent your uncle the second time, you knew it was just the battery, and it was already fixed."

He looked down at his cone, studying it far too intently. "I guess."

Josh rested his fingers on Bradley's little arm. "I'm not mad at you, Bradley. I just want you to know that it's not very nice to do stuff like that. And speaking of not nice, I'd like to know why you had me go to the school three days in a row like that. I know I tightened your thermos lid, and I could be very mad at you for wrecking your good lunch. Why did you want me to go to the school? You didn't seem like you wanted to talk to me. I ended up talking to Miss Klassen every time."

"Didn't you like talking to Miss Klassen?" He turned to Melissa. "You had fun talking to Uncle Josh, didn't you?"

"Of course," Melissa and Josh said in unison.

Bradley's face lit up like a Christmas tree. "See?"

Josh cleared his throat, and Melissa continued to watch.

"No, Bradley, I don't see."

"You like Miss Klassen, don't you? She's nice and smart and pretty and everything."

Melissa felt her cheeks heat up.

"Yes, Miss Klassen is very nice," Josh replied.

Suddenly, Bradley turned to Melissa. "And you like Uncle Josh, right? He's really smart, and he's a great mechanic, and he cooks good too."

The heat in her cheeks climbed a few degrees as she wondered how she could reply and keep a little dignity. "Yes, Bradley, that's right."

Bradley resumed eating his ice cream cone. "See? Mom and Dad said that part of being a good parent means doing some adult stuff without us, and they sometimes went out to restaurants by themselves. And they were always so happy when they came back. So since you're trying to be a good parent with Mom and Dad gone, you should go to restaurants and stuff too. Except you don't have a girlfriend anymore, and since Miss Klassen doesn't have a boyfriend, and since you're both so nice, then you two should go out and do adult stuff."

He stopped eating the ice cream again, and looked back and forth between the two of them. An emotion Melissa couldn't define emanated from his big brown eyes, so sad for a little boy, yet pleading at the same time.

Bradley's voice lowered to barely above a whisper. "Just

like Mom and Dad."

Melissa's heart clenched. That Bradley truly did not have a crush on her suddenly came as no consolation. Not in light of what was really on his mind.

Josh cleared his throat. "So you think that I should go out with Miss Klassen, just like your mom and dad went out?"

Bradley nodded. "Yes. So you can be happy. I want you to be happy, Uncle Josh. Sometimes you don't look very happy." He turned to Melissa. "And you too, Miss Klassen. Are you happy when you go do stuff with Uncle Josh?"

Melissa nearly choked. She couldn't define how she felt when she did "stuff" with Josh. All she did know was that being with Josh felt different than when she had dated other men, probably because it wasn't a dating relationship, even though she didn't know what to call it.

"But Bradley, Miss Klassen and I aren't married like your mom and dad. It's different."

He nodded again. "I know. Then it's called a date. You're supposed to go out and do dates until you get married. That's how it works."

Melissa didn't think she needed a six year old to tell her how her social life and romantic relationships were supposed to work. "Uncle Josh is right, Bradley. It's different than with your mom and dad."

"I know. You gotta be in love when you're married. But when you're just in like, that's why you date. Cody splained it to me, so I know all about dating. Cody's mom is dating Erica's dad. They like each other really lots. You like Uncle Josh really lots, don't you?"

Melissa felt the walls closing in around her. "Well, yes. . ."

Bradley turned to Josh. Josh's face paled. "You like Miss Klassen really lots, don't you, Uncle Josh?"

"Well, yes. . ."

Bradley grinned from ear to ear. "See? I was right. That's why you gotta do dating. That's what Cody said about dating."

Melissa knew Cody. He was also in her class at school.

Cody had a lot to learn about love and dating before he started "splaining" the intricacies of romantic relationships to his classmates, especially classmates who were looking for difficult answers.

"So," Bradley mumbled as he rammed the entire bottom of his ice cream cone into his mouth, "are you taking Miss Klassen on a date on Friday? Tyler already said he'd baby-sit."

"But. . . ," Josh stammered. "I don't know. . ."

Melissa couldn't handle watching Bradley's excitement turning to disappointment. In this situation, Josh was in far over his head and needed someone to talk to, without being in Bradley's presence. For the sake of the boy, who had far more to deal with than she ever had as a child, she could endure a real "date" with his uncle, even if all they did this time was talk seriously about what they were going to do about Bradley.

"Yes, Bradley," Melissa said. "I do believe your uncle and I have a date Friday night, don't we, Uncle Josh?"

Josh stared at her with his mouth hanging open, then snapped it shut. He turned and glanced quickly at Bradley, then turned back to her. "Yes, Miss Klassen, I believe we do. Oh, by the way, did you know your ice cream is melting down your arm?"

eleven

Melissa's heart pounded as she opened the door.

"Hi," she mumbled.

"Hi, yourself." Josh smiled, and her heart went wild.

This time, it wasn't just dinner after a shopping excursion. This time, it was a real date. She knew it was real because Josh was wearing a tie that matched a neatly pressed shirt, and he wore fitted slacks instead of jeans. He had also shaved, and his hair didn't show telltale specks of grease at the end of a workday, so he had recently showered.

"You look n-nice," she stammered.

"You look very nice too. That blue looks really good on you. It's the same color as your eyes."

She didn't want to know that he'd paid any attention to the color of her eyes. She forced herself to smile and hoped it appeared genuine. "Thanks. It's the same blue as your coveralls."

"That was what I didn't need to hear. I'm finished with coveralls until Monday at nine A.M. Where would you like to go?"

"I don't know. Someplace really quiet would be a good idea."

"Does that mean you want to sit across from each other at a cozy table for two where soft, romantic music plays in the background, and the flickering candlelight will hypnotize us as we stare into each other's eyes across the barely lit table?"

Melissa felt all the color drain from her face.

Josh dragged his hand over his face. "Sorry. I'm not handling this very well. I still can't believe Bradley's done it again, but it's even worse than last time. Not only did a kid set me up for a date, twice now, this time he also picked what he wanted me to wear and laid everything out on the bed for

123

me when I got home from work." He spread his arms at his sides. "He picked my best clothes, and then he made me wear the tie."

His frustration made her smile, and her breathing returned to normal. "I think Bradley did a wonderful job dressing you."

"Yeah. Well, since we're both all dressed up, it would seem a shame to waste his efforts. Let's go somewhere nice, just not too romantic. You know the neighborhood better than I do. You pick."

"How about that new steak house by the arena? I forget the name, but you seem to like steak. Have you ever been there before? It's not exactly in the neighborhood, but I can recommend it, and we're dressed for it."

"Sounds good to me. You ready?"

Melissa pulled a light coat out of the closet, locked up, and walked with Josh to the street, where he opened the door of the van and waited for her to get in.

She grinned as she pushed herself up and in. "I've never gone on a date in a minivan before."

"Don't remind me. I still can't believe I'm doing this. I don't mean going out with you—I mean this way."

Melissa chattered about anything other than children and cars all the way to the restaurant, while Josh remained silent most of the time.

Fortunately, by the time they were seated at a table, he had relaxed into the Josh she was used to.

Since the steak house was filled almost to capacity with a variety of couples, families, and other groups, the atmosphere was nothing like the romantic setting he had teased her about earlier.

Watching him as he smiled and commented at something she said, she wondered what a romantic date with Josh would be like. On the heels of that thought, she tried not to regret that an outing such as the one he'd described in jest would never happen in seriousness, even if she were in a position to really begin such a relationship with him.

Melissa couldn't help it. Despite Bradley's blunt questions, she did like Josh. She liked his easygoing nature, yet at the same time he was incredibly responsible. On the surface, his carefree and relaxed demeanor made him appear no different than any other single twenty-five-year-old man, but Melissa knew otherwise.

A list of his good qualities—in addition to a few very endearing flaws—formulated in her mind. If she didn't know any better, she could have thought she was falling in love with him.

Melissa nearly choked on her salad.

"Melissa? Are you okay? Want my water?"

She accepted his water without comment and sipped it until the tightness in her throat loosened. His concern and quick action only made her dilemma worse.

They managed to keep the conversation light throughout their dinner until the waitress removed their plates and they were left to talk without distractions.

Josh cleared his throat and wiggled the knot of his tie. "I guess we should talk about Bradley and stuff."

"Stuff?"

"You know. Stuff." His voice dropped to a husky mumble. "Us." He cleared his throat again. "What are we going to do?"

"I don't know. I don't want to cause Bradley any more stress or anxiety. His heart is in the right place."

"I know. I nearly lost it when he said all he was trying to do was to make me happy. I didn't know I looked unhappy to him."

"Besides the normal day-to-day stress of living with them when it's like nothing you've ever experienced in your life, is there anything that he was referring to?"

His face whitened slightly, and he suddenly began to rearrange the teaspoon and dessert fork in front of him. "Yeah. There is."

"I'm sorry, Josh," she stammered. "I didn't mean to pry. Forget that I asked."

"No," Josh mumbled. "He said it right in front of you anyway, so I might as tell you about it. For the last three years, I've been going steady with a woman. I even thought we could get married. We recently split up. That's probably what he's thinking of."

Her chest tightened so badly it hurt. "Is there any chance of reconciliation?"

He shook his head, not looking up as he continued to play with the silverware. "No. Bradley doesn't know this—none of the kids do, and they never will. She left me because of the kids."

"What?"

"We talked about me moving in with them and being their legal guardian beforehand, even though my mind was already made up. She was against the idea from the start, but I couldn't not take the kids, not under the circumstances. When I moved into Brian and Sasha's house, she supposedly tried to make it work and get used to me living with the kids, but it only lasted for exactly two weeks, and she said she couldn't do it."

He paused, but Melissa didn't know what he expected her to say, if anything. Two weeks wasn't nearly long enough to become accustomed to such a situation, and it certainly wasn't long enough to figure out how to deal with the changes that would become necessary. His awkwardness gave her the impression he hadn't yet talked about what happened to anyone and that he needed to get it out of his system.

She folded her hands on the table in front of her. "What happened?"

"First she said that I wasn't spending enough time with her. Then when I did spend time with her, most of the time I was so exhausted I was falling asleep. She didn't like coming over because she thought the kids were suffocating her, but they only wanted some attention, which was understandable at the time. Brian warned me about that, and I told Theresa what Brian said. I didn't want to go out for awhile because I didn't want to leave them with a sitter, except for the short amount of time from when they get off school until Tyler gets home. I couldn't make Tyler baby-sit more than that at first. He was pretty mad at life for a few weeks. I didn't want to add to it. I certainly wasn't going to hire a sitter just to take off and have some fun. Not just after I moved in. It wouldn't have been right."

"It sounds like you were doing the right thing."

"I thought so, but Theresa said I was ignoring her, that I was always busy with the kids, and that's probably true. No, not probably. It is true. I never knew how hard it would be to be a single parent. I know I put the kids first. I had to. Right now, those kids are the most important things in my life, and they're going to be for a long time. She was mad because everything I did centered around them and not her."

"But those things tend to level off if you give it awhile. Look at how much time I've spent with you in the last couple of weeks. Everything looks fine now, at least it does to me."

"It is, but it took about a month for the boys and me to get used to each other. I guess Theresa didn't see that it could change. Either that, or she didn't want to. Without going into details, I'll just say that our parting wasn't done on kind words. She wanted to do the white picket fence thing with me. You know, get married, have fun for awhile, get a house, and then have one or two kids. You know, make some babies of our own."

His face flushed, which Melissa thought rather sweet.

Josh cleared his throat but didn't look up. "Raising five kids from six to fifteen years old is different, even if they are family. Even you said you'd never want to have five kids even if they were your own, never mind someone else's."

"I didn't say that."

He raised his head, and the sadness in his eyes nearly broke her heart. "Yes, you did. I wasn't mistaken, because when Theresa dumped me, she said the same thing."

She was about to say he was wrong, but her protest caught in her throat. She had said that, but she certainly hadn't meant it that way. At the time, she had been asking him about why he suddenly took on five children, and they had been talking about how the boys were adjusting to their new home life, and the difficulties in raising five children in general.

Suddenly, the dessert the waitress placed in front of her held no appeal.

Before she could think of something to say, Josh started to speak.

"I don't know why I told you all that," he said, mumbling as he picked at his cheesecake with the fork, not eating his dessert, either. "This has nothing to do with figuring out what we're going to do about Bradley."

On the contrary, Melissa thought it did. It explained why Bradley thought Josh was unhappy, and most of all, it told her that while on the surface Josh was fine, deep down he really was as unhappy as Bradley said. Now she knew why.

As well, something happened in her heart, and she knew that if she wasn't sure if she loved him before, she knew without a doubt now.

Melissa was in love with Josh McMillian, single guardian of five active boys. Five boys who had unintentionally erected a shield around their uncle's heart of gold.

She laid down the fork and folded her hands on the table to address Josh with more authority. "I think Bradley is doing this for two reasons. First, he sees the going out thing as something his parents did. The way he's relating you to their routine suggests to me that he's accepted you completely as his substitute parent. So that's really good. Secondly, he sees that when his parents went out they came back happy, and he wants you to be happy too. It's obviously important to him that you're happy, Josh."

"Yeah. I know. It stung at the time when Theresa dumped me, but I'm over it. I really am."

"I don't think Bradley thinks the same way, or he would be satisfied to have you be single and spend that time with him. But I have an idea. I don't mind if you want to go out every once in while and let Bradley think we're dating, but we can just see each other as friends. I don't want to make you commit to something that you're not in a position to do. I know the boys come first, and that's the way it should be. If Bradley sees us doing what he perceives as dating, it will help him deal with life. I wouldn't want to see him go through what he did before. It nearly broke my heart watching him try to sort things out. I'm also sure the other boys have had similar adjustments to make too."

"Yes, they've all had their stuff to sort out in their heads."

"Let's just give it some time. When Bradley has everything figured out, we can either pretend to split up, or we can simply go out less and less and let it peter out."

"You mean pretend to date? You'd be okay with that? It just occurred to me that I never asked if you're seeing someone right now. It's rather obvious I'm not."

Melissa picked up the fork and pushed a strawberry around on the plate. "Don't worry. I'm not seeing anyone."

She didn't stop playing with her dessert, but she did glance up without moving her head to see that Josh was now doing the same thing with his dessert.

"That's good," he muttered, then raised his head. "No, I didn't mean it like that. What I mean to say is that I'm glad that whatever it is we're doing isn't going to come between you and someone else and interfere with an existing relationship. Actually, I've thought about that often since Bradley has been putting us together, before we knew what he was doing. Even though I'm sorry to hear that you don't have anyone to call special, I'm glad I'm not causing some kind of problem. You know what I mean."

"Yes, I do know what you mean. You have nothing to worry about."

"I think this could work, but I worry that you have better things to do with your evenings than to waste your time going out with me."

She had at least a hundred reasons why she wanted to go

out with him. She also had a hundred reasons why she shouldn't. However, she wasn't going to let the negative over-power the positive.

From the way her heart soared when she saw Josh, even knowing he didn't feel the same way, she didn't think she would be seeing anyone else for a long time. She would never find anyone like Josh, ever again. If she didn't see him like this, as friends with the guidelines they'd set, she wouldn't see him at all, and she couldn't handle that.

"I'm always in the market for a new friend. I really don't do much most evenings except for Bible study night."

He smiled, and the butterflies in her stomach went to war with the nice steak dinner she'd just eaten.

"I'd like that. I think I need a friend right now." He reached across the table and covered her hands with his. "Thank you, Melissa. You'll never know how much this means to me."

And he would never know how much their friendship meant to her.

Melissa felt the backs of her eyes burn, but she blinked it away. "Don't worry about it. Everything will work out just fine. But I think it's time to go. I guess I'll see you next time at church on Sunday."

They both stood.

"Yes. I might as well ask you now. Do you want to come over for lunch?"

⋰

Josh knocked on Melissa's door and checked his watch. As much as he enjoyed his time out with Melissa, he didn't have time for this. They'd made it a habit to go out twice during the week besides the Bible study, plus once on the weekend. Tonight they had decided to go to a movie, but he should have been at home helping Kyle with his homework. In addition to that, he also should have been fixing the loose board in the fence that Andrew had accidentally knocked out with the soc-cer ball. Or, he could also have chosen tonight to try and unclog the sink in the downstairs bathroom, which once full, took seven minutes and sixteen seconds to drain. The boys had timed it with the stopwatch feature on Ryan's wristwatch. They thought they were having fun, squealing with glee when the last drop finally disappeared out of sight and they hit the stop button. It only reminded Josh of one more job he had to do.

"Hi, Josh. You look tired."

"Yeah, I am tired, but that's okay. I've been tired before, I'll be tired again. How are you doing? The little kids run you off your feet again today?"

She smiled, and a little of the weight seemed to lift off Josh's shoulders. "No, today was pretty quiet. Or as quiet as can be when surrounded by six and seven year olds all day."

He sauntered in and flopped down on the couch. "Better you than me. I figure we should leave in fifteen minutes if we want to get a good seat."

"I just have some stuff to take out of the dryer. If I fold it, then I won't have to iron as much. Do you mind waiting? Just turn on the TV, and I'll be only a few minutes."

"Take your time. As long as it's not longer than fifteen minutes."

She stuck her tongue out at him and gave him the raspberries as she left the room. Josh grinned back, then started to search for the remote.

He couldn't believe how quickly they'd fallen into an easy friendship, which was exactly what he needed. He hadn't realized how much he'd missed the simple pleasure of being able to be completely at ease with a person. Even after dating Theresa for three years, it hadn't been like this. He didn't know if he could even be this way with his best friend, whom he hadn't seen in three months, and probably wouldn't see for another three months if things kept up the way they were.

With a flick of a button, a popular sitcom came on. Josh slouched and stuck his legs out straight in front of him as he stretched out to relax. He'd already seen this episode, or rather, he'd heard it while he was busy doing something else a couple of days ago, but he didn't have the energy to reach over and grab the remote a second time.

Since he already knew what was going to happen, Josh let his eyes drift shut, just to give himself a few minutes to think of how he might unclog the drain without having to take the pipe apart and pick the slime out of the trap, a job he wasn't looking forward to doing. He wondered if he might make a trip to the hardware store on the way home, if it was still open, and just buy a new trap piece and outright replace it. Or maybe he could think of another way. . . .

Slowly, his thoughts faded into oblivion as the voices from the television droned on.

twelve

"Josh? Josh?"

A slight shaking on his right shoulder brought Josh back to the land of the living. "Huh? What?" He opened one eye. "Melissa?"

He let his head flop back on the couch. "I fell asleep, didn't I?"

"Isn't that a rhetorical question?"

If he'd been more alert, he would have bugged her about answering a question with a question, but he knew that in his sleep-fogged state, a battle of wits against a teacher was a losing proposition.

"No, just a dumb question. What time is it?"

"It's nearly nine, and time for you to go home."

He sat up straight, then felt himself sway with the too-fast movement. "I slept for two hours? I'm so sorry. You should have kicked me or something."

Her smile jolted him the rest of the way to full wakefulness. "Naw. I got all my ironing done, did some dusting, and I got caught up in some prep work for school tomorrow. I was going to go in early to do it, but I did it tonight instead. Now I can sleep in a little later. Oh, I also got some reading done. I recently joined the Heartsong Presents book club, and I get four great little Christian romance novels every month. So it wasn't like I had nothing to do."

"In other words, you worked around me."

"Something like that. Did you know you snore?"

Josh's cheeks burned. "I do not."

"You do."

He covered his face with his hands. "I'm so sorry. I guess I'm not a very fun date. And when I get home, the kids are going to ask what we did tonight."

"Tell them we spent a very quiet evening together instead of the movie."

He dropped his hands and grinned. "It wasn't that quiet if I snore."

Her answering grin did funny things to his insides. Josh covered his stomach with his open palms. "Have you got anything to eat? I think I'm hungry or something."

"You may choose between an apple, a banana, or a carrot."

"I'll take the carrot. Gotta have my 'vegabulls.' Thanks."

"At least you practice what you preach."

He followed her into the kitchen, then waited while she washed and peeled it for him.

"I could have done that myself," he mumbled as he bit into the carrot. "But thanks anyway."

"I'm sure you could have washed and peeled it. But I did it for you. I was being nice."

If it were anyone else, he would have made a snide comment, but he couldn't with Melissa. She really was nice, not just on the surface but from the depths of her being. If it wasn't for needing to expend all his time and energy on Bradley and the other kids, he would have dated her for real, and not be bound by their wacky arrangement to be friends, and friends only. On the other hand, if it wasn't for Bradley and his childish matchmaking efforts, he wouldn't have met her at all.

Either way he looked at it, it was a lose-lose situation.

Instead of saying what he really thought, Josh decided to change the subject. "I think going out three times on the weeknights is too much for this tired, old man. Obviously you're busy too, and seeing me is taking time away from stuff that's really important. Do you think we should start to cut down the amount of time we're going out on these dates? I think one date during the week, plus Bible study night, then once on the weekend is enough for Bradley to see us together."

Her eyes widened, and her voice came out quieter than usual. "Sure. We've been doing this for a few weeks. I think we can start to cut back."

Her quick agreement gave him little consolation. He had wanted her to argue with him, and when she hadn't, he felt disappointed.

Josh shook his head. Part of him wanted to keep seeing her four days a week, because he had to count Sunday morning as well as Bible study meeting along with their scheduled date nights. The sensible part of him knew it was too much—he couldn't keep it up. Still, he wanted her to protest.

Since she hadn't, and it was for the best anyway, as soon as Josh finished eating the carrot, he headed for home.

Instead of silence, which he should have heard when he opened the door since it was after bedtime on a school night, Josh opened the front door to a myriad of screaming.

"What's going on in here?" he bellowed as he closed the door behind him and pushed Cleo aside, hoping the volume of his voice would carry over the rest of them, and they'd suddenly become quiet.

They didn't. He stood in the hall, trying to figure out where in the house they were while he tried to stop Cleo from jumping on him. "Where are you guys?" he called.

"Ryan won't give me my Proton Battlezoid!"

"Your Battlezoid is stupid!"

"No, you're stupid!"

The screaming turned to wailing at the sound of a resounding smack.

Josh ran into the den and pulled Ryan and Kyle apart. "What are you two doing? You're supposed to be in bed! Quit this fighting!"

The second he released them, before Josh could do anything about it, Kyle rushed forward and punched his brother in the stomach. Ryan kicked Kyle in the shin before Josh could intervene.

He pulled them apart, keeping the struggling, screaming

children at full arm's lengths on both sides until they stopped moving, at which point Josh released them, this time being better prepared if they went at it again.

"That does it, you two. I don't know what started this, but it's over. For your punishments, you're both going to do dishes for three days, and you're going to go straight to your room after school tomorrow and clean everything up perfect. No friends, no TV, and no video games or computer until I say it's good enough."

The tears streamed faster down Ryan's cheeks, and he didn't say a word, but Kyle turned to Josh, his face beet red, and stomped one foot.

"You can't make me do that!" he screamed. "You're not my dad, and I don't have to do what you say. Soon Mom and Dad will be back, and they'll show you! Come on, Ryan. Let's go!"

Both boys ran off side by side, leaving Josh standing in the den with his mouth hanging open, feeling poleaxed like a cop in a domestic dispute.

Before he could piece together what had just happened and figure out what he should do about such an act of defiance, Tyler sauntered in, eating a cup of instant noodles.

Josh turned to Tyler. "Where were you while this was going on? Didn't you hear them fighting?"

Tyler stuffed a forkful of noodles into his mouth. "Sorry," he mumbled around his mouthful. "The kettle was boiling, and I had my head in the fridge. I guess I didn't hear."

Josh wanted to take Tyler to task for not adequately supervising, but held off. He didn't know if he should have been expecting Tyler to be able to ward off such squabbles when he'd been leaving them alone so much. In doing what he could to help Bradley deal with the separation from his parents, he didn't want to blow it with Tyler. He didn't know exactly how Ryan felt, but he knew he'd lost a lot of ground with Kyle today.

Josh sucked in a deep breath to compose himself. He needed time to think, but first he had to see that all the younger ones were in bed. "Where are Bradley and Andrew?"

"Bradley's in bed," mumbled Tyler around another huge forkful of noodles. "Andrew's on the computer."

"It's nearly nine thirty. Why weren't Ryan and Kyle in bed? Andrew should be getting to bed too."

"Sorry. I was on the phone with Allyson until just a couple of minutes ago. I guess I didn't notice the time. How was the movie?"

"We didn't go to the movie. We spent a quiet evening at her place."

Tyler's eyes widened. "Really? Wow. . ."

"Trust me, Tyler, we did nothing. Absolutely nothing. It was a very quiet evening."

"Is this thing with Bradley's teacher, like, you know, serious?"

Josh tried not to cringe or show any sign of nervousness. "Why do you ask?"

"I dunno. I think she's really nice. I like her a lot better than Theresa. You two seem, like, okay. I just don't know what to call her. Should I call her Miss Klassen or Melissa?"

The funny thing was, he knew exactly what Tyler meant. Josh smiled. "Sometimes I don't know what to call her either, Tyler."

"I guess it depends if Bradley or the little kids are around."

"Exactly."

Tyler shrugged his shoulders. "Want me to tell Andrew to get ready for bed?"

"Yes. I'm going to have to deal with Ryan and Kyle. And then you get to bed too, okay?"

Tyler grunted, so Josh assumed the response was affirmative. He gathered up his courage and walked into Ryan and Kyle's bedroom. The light was already out. The boys weren't quiet, but the second he walked in, all shuffling stopped.

"Do you guys have something to say to each other?"

"Sorry," they both muttered, not at all sounding like either of them meant it.

Both Ryan and Kyle had regular single beds, allowing Josh to sit down on the side of Kyle's bed and talk to them both on a level playing field.

"Kyle, I want to talk to you about what you said earlier."

"I'm sorry, Uncle Josh. I didn't mean it. I know you're in charge of us while Mom and Dad are gone. Are you still going to punish us?"

"Yes, Kyle, I still have to punish you because you still said it, and you still hit your brother. And Ryan, you were equally to blame. I don't want to know who started it. A fight is only a fight if two people are in it. One person can't fight alone."

He took their silence as agreement, although he doubted this would be the last time they held this same conversation. It certainly wasn't the first.

"I also want to talk to you about your mom and dad. Kyle, your mom and dad told you that it would be a long time until they came back. The soonest they will be back will be at Easter time, not this Easter, but next Easter. When you're in grade seven."

"I know. They really are coming back, aren't they, Uncle Josh?"

"Yes, Kyle, they really are coming back."

"What will you do when Mom and Dad come back? Are you still gonna live with us?"

"No, I won't. I'll go live by myself again."

"What about Miss Klassen?"

"She'll still live by herself, just like she does now."

A silence hung in the air. He thought he probably should have said something more about Melissa, but he didn't know what Kyle was really asking, or what he needed to hear.

"Okay, it's bedtime. Would you like to say bedtime prayers now? I think it's Ryan's turn first tonight."

He listened to their prayers, and it soothed his worries to some degree when they both asked to be forgiven for all the sins they did that day, although Josh doubted they really understood the broad definition of being a sinner.

"Amen," he said when Kyle was done. He stood and gave them both a short hug, tucked them in, and left them to sleep.

His next stop was Andrew and Bradley's room, where Andrew had the top bunk, and Bradley slept below. Bradley's deep, even breathing told Josh that he had been asleep for a long time. Andrew had just scaled the ladder and was settling the blankets around himself.

"Hey, Andrew. Wanna say prayers?"

"Okay."

He watched Andrew close his eyes, fold his hands on his stomach, take a deep breath, and then relax. Being thirteen, he liked Josh to be there when he said his prayers. He just didn't want anyone to listen to his private thoughts and wishes, and Josh had to respect that.

"Amen," Andrew said when he was done.

"Amen," Josh echoed.

Josh reached over the side rail and patted Andrew on the shoulder. Andrew thought he was too big for hugging, but he still appreciated a gentle touch at bedtime. Josh could remember being thirteen. It was when he realized that he hadn't been exactly planned, giving him a few personal struggles worrying his parents didn't really want him. He'd also started attending youth group with a friend, a time in his life he would never forget. Even at such a young age, he understood the love of God in his life and reached for it almost desperately. But being thirteen, he also didn't want anyone to see his anxieties. The experience made him very sensitive to Andrew's moods and taught him not to brush off Andrew's sometimes veiled questions, as a deeper meaning often lurked below.

"Good night, Andrew," he whispered loudly as he headed toward the door.

"Uncle Josh?"

"Yes, Andrew?"

"Did you have fun tonight?"

He wouldn't have exactly called it fun, but he hadn't had a

bad time. Again, he suspected there was more to Andrew's question than the obvious response, but he couldn't think of anything profound to say. "Yes, I had fun."

He waited for either a response or a clarification to the real meaning of Andrew's question, but there was none forthcoming.

"Okay. Good night, Uncle Josh."

"Good night, Andrew," he repeated, and slipped out the door.

The last stop was Tyler's room. Being the oldest, Tyler didn't have to share, which was not necessarily a bad thing. From the amount of junk and paraphernalia constantly littering the furniture, then spilling onto the carpet, Josh doubted there would have been room to put a second person with Tyler.

"You sleeping yet?" he asked as he poked his head in the door.

"Almost. Good night, Uncle Josh."

Josh closed the door, then leaned his back against the wall. Josh couldn't intrude into Tyler's private time when he crawled into bed. He didn't know if Tyler said prayers at night, or anytime. He couldn't supervise or guide him in the process of learning how to talk to God but had to rely on youth group meetings and by being a good example and hoping it would rub off.

Josh didn't like doing it that way, but he didn't have a choice. If he could have started with Tyler younger, he would have had more opportunity to guide him. Now, he could only do the best he could by example.

Josh wasn't sure how good an example he could be. He didn't know enough about kids to be able to read them properly.

One thing he had noticed tonight was that all of them except for Bradley had asked about his relationship with Melissa rather than asking specifically about her personally. He couldn't tell if it was curiosity, or they were all seeking a permanent relationship to relate to in the absence of the steadying nearness of their mother and father, like he knew Bradley was.

The thought of being put in such a position terrified him.

He'd recently had a talk with Melissa about her principal, in other words, her boss. Principal Swain had a reasonable concern to request that teachers not date parents, or guardians, in his case, as part of their code of conduct, but in real life, things weren't so black and white.

While Josh didn't fully agree, he understood the risk she was taking to continue to see him and appreciated it. She had no worries about him cheating on a wife or significant other, but he did understand the possibility of children seeing favoritism, even when there was none. So far nothing had been said, but Melissa told him she'd noticed gossip about her keeping company with Bradley McMillian's uncle starting to rear its ugly head.

He didn't know what to do. He didn't want her to get in trouble, nor did he want to be the case of dissension in her classroom, where she had to be perceived as the ultimate authority to the children, but he didn't want to stop seeing her, either.

It left him no choice but to tell her that when the time came to make a decision on what to do, the decision would be completely up to her. If that decision came down to not seeing him again, he would have to accept that.

Josh's stomach started to feel a little strange, so he headed into the kitchen to make himself a snack. As he constructed a sandwich to die for, the thought occurred to him that ever since he'd met Melissa, he'd been eating more. For a second he rested one hand on his stomach, just to make sure that he hadn't been putting on any weight, then carried his sandwich into the living room. Instead of flipping on the television, Josh dug out his guide to reading the Bible in a year, and prepared to catch up on a couple of days, exactly what he needed for tonight.

Tomorrow was another day.

❧

Josh wasn't surprised that none of the kids were in bed when he got home. He always gave them plenty of leeway for bedtime on Saturday night, partly as a bribe to convince them to go to church Sunday morning with no argument, and partly because at the end of the week, he simply didn't have the energy to fight with them anymore.

What he hadn't expected was to see them all waiting for him the second he stepped inside the door.

"Why are you home so early, Uncle Josh?"

"Did you have fun, Uncle Josh?"

"Is Miss Klassen going to be at church tomorrow, Uncle Josh?"

"Where did you go, Uncle Josh? Did you have pizza again?"

"When are you going to see Miss Klassen next time, Uncle Josh?"

Josh raised his hands in the air to silence them, but all that happened was that Cleo jumped up and nearly knocked the breath out of him with her paws in his stomach. "Hold on, you guys! Why all the questions?"

Bradley stepped forward. "You didn't go out with Miss Klassen last week. Don't you like her anymore? Was today okay?"

Josh's stomach did a strange flip. This time he knew he wasn't hungry because he and Melissa had just eaten not long ago.

Last weekend they'd had "the talk." Nothing had been said to her directly, but her principal had called her into his office and warned her about a minor infraction. The offense was so minor that it should have been ignored, but in a way she had not been surprised.

It had started. Principal Swain didn't have the grounds to reprimand her for anything she did in her personal life, but this had been his way of showing her that he had learned she was going against his mandate by seeing Josh. They'd discussed taking it to her union as harassment, but since they'd been "dating" for a number of months, they had already been on the verge of their decision to cut back to weekends only and seeing if the boys noticed.

Apparently they noticed.

"Of course I still like her. We just thought we wouldn't see each other so often. Now get to bed."

The room became so quiet all he could hear was Cleo's panting. Then, in the blink of an eye, they all were gone.

Josh smiled. It didn't happen often, but sometimes he won.

thirteen

Melissa pulled over to the side of the road, then fumbled in her purse for her ringing cell phone.

"Hello?"

"Miss Klassen? Is that you? You sound funny."

Melissa had never received a call from a child on her cell phone before, but she had a good idea who it was.

"Bradley? Is that you?"

"No. It's me, Ryan. Bradley's not home."

Melissa's heart pounded. She didn't know how Ryan got her number, but there could only be one reason for Ryan to be calling her on the cell phone. Another disaster had befallen the McMillian family, and they couldn't find Josh.

Suddenly she became very glad she had pulled to the side of the road to answer the phone, because her hands were shaking so much she could barely hold the phone, never mind drive without running into something. She tried to keep her voice steady. "What's wrong, Ryan? Where's your uncle Josh?"

"He went to the store with Bradley to get something, but I gotta do my homework, and I'm stuck."

She highly doubted anything he could have been assigned for grade three was that difficult or that any of his brothers wouldn't be able to assist him. "Where is everybody else? Isn't Tyler home? Can't anyone else help you?"

"But you used to be my teacher when I was in grade one, so you know this better than them."

She also doubted that Josh and Bradley would be gone long on a school night, which made her wonder about the real reason for Ryan's call.

There was only one way to find out. She checked her watch. "I can be there in about ten minutes."

"That's great, Miss Klassen. Thanks. Bye."

Rather than go home, she turned and headed for the McMillian house.

She raised her fist to knock, but the door opened before she made contact. Before she did anything, she bent to pat Cleo before Cleo jumped on her.

"Why did you bring food, Miss Klassen? I only asked for help with my homework. Uncle Josh already bought lots of food yesterday."

"I was on my way home from grocery shopping, so I need to put a few things in your freezer while I'm here."

"Oh."

Tyler appeared beside Ryan with the cordless phone attached to his ear. "I'll put that away for you."

Before she could protest, Tyler removed the bag from her hands and hustled away.

"Okay, Ryan, let me see this homework problem."

After eight minutes the problem was solved. "Is there anything else, Ryan?"

Ryan frantically turned the pages in his notebook. "I don't know. I think so. But I can't find it. Math is really hard. Just a minute. I know I can find it."

A chorus of frantic barking echoed from the living room.

"Uncle Josh!" Ryan hollered and bolted from the room. Rather than sit all alone in Ryan and Kyle's bedroom, she followed Ryan to the door.

"Hey, Cleo," she heard Josh say. "Ryan, that looks like Miss Klassen's car in front."

"Miss Klassen is here, Uncle Josh! She came to help with my homework!"

"Your homework? But. . . ," his voice trailed off as she rounded the corner into the entranceway. "Melissa? What are you doing here?"

She tried to keep a straight face. "I was just on my way home, and I received a very frantic call on my cell phone from a little boy very anxious to finish his homework."

Josh glared at Ryan, whose little face had turned very red. "Homework, Ryan?"

"Yeah. It was real hard, but Miss Klassen helped me. I gotta go pick up my toys. Bye."

In the blink of an eye, Ryan and Bradley, who had been silent the entire time, disappeared, leaving Melissa and Josh alone beside the front door.

Josh turned his head, staring at the deserted doorway to the living room where the boys had exited. "I think something is rotten in the state of Denmark," he muttered.

She could no longer hold it back. Melissa allowed her laughter to break free. Josh didn't even crack a smile.

"Oh, come on, Josh," she said through her giggles. "You've got to admit that was pretty good."

"Not really. I wonder where they learn such stuff from? I'm going to have to monitor what they're watching on television a little closer."

Finally, she managed to keep a straight face. "Forget it, Josh. While I'm here, we might as well make the best of it. Are you going to make me some coffee, or do I have to make it myself?"

She tried not to laugh again as she followed Josh into the kitchen, grumbling every step of the way.

"Tell me what you had to get at the store for Bradley."

"It wasn't a big thing. He broke a shoelace, and he can't go to school tomorrow without laces in one shoe, so I had to run out and buy a shoelace. Strange, though, that it broke right where it was too short to make do for a day or two."

She sat at the kitchen table while Josh ran the water to start the coffee. She plunked her elbows on the table and cradled her chin in her palms, biting her lip so he couldn't see her grin. "Really? Don't you think that's a bit strange?"

"Hmm. . . Now that you mention it, I can't remember ever breaking a lace at that age. I wore out my shoes long before the laces gave out."

"Yes, it's pretty amazing, isn't it?"

"Oh, well, I have more important things to worry about than broken shoelaces. I got an E-mail from Brian today."

All the humor of the situation dissipated. "Is it good or bad?"

"A little of both, actually. He said Sasha's responding well to treatment, but she still has a lot of progress to make. I got really mixed feelings from his message. On one hand it was really encouraging, but at the same time it was a reminder of how far she has to go and how long this could take. Brian sounded both encouraged and discouraged at the same time. I didn't know how to respond."

Every Bible study meeting, either Melissa or Josh had brought forward Sasha's condition and Brian's struggles to help his wife as a weekly prayer concern, as well as everything Josh had to deal with in taking over the everyday running of the household and family. This time, Josh needed a little extra help and support in trying to be encouraging to his brother, who was having a tough time. "Would you like to pray about it?"

He flipped the switch to start the coffee brewing, and turned to stand in front of her while she remained seated. "Yes, actually, I would. Thanks." His voice dropped to barely above a whisper. "I'd like to go into the den and close the door. I don't want the kids to interrupt; you know what their timing is like. I also don't want them to hear us. After all, we'll be praying for their parents, and I don't want to have to edit my prayers for their ears today."

She glanced to the opening between the kitchen and the living room, listening to the usual activities and the mayhem that accompanied it. "Yes, that's a good idea."

Without drawing the point that they didn't want to be disturbed to the boys' attention, Melissa quietly followed Josh into the den.

At the sound of the snick of the lock, a bad case of the jitters attacked her sensibilities. They prayed together often, not just at the weekly Bible study meetings, but also in private at her house. They were less alone here behind the locked door with the boys running around than they were at her house in the wide open spaces of the living room or kitchen. Somehow, this felt. . .different.

She didn't know why now, of all times, she was letting him affect her like this. This was Josh. Over the past few months they had developed a friendship unlike any other she'd experienced in her life.

Not long after they'd met, she once had the cockamamie idea that she'd fallen in love with him. However, Josh never indicated to her anything other than pure friendship, both in receiving and in the many ways he gave of himself to her. It didn't take long for her to come to her senses and tell herself that it wasn't really love.

Love was excitement and fireworks. She'd never experienced any of that kind of thing with Josh. He'd never been romantic in any way. Over time they had become almost a daily part of each other's lives, together for ordinary, normal day-to-day happenings, taking the ups with the downs. Instead of the tender affection she expected in a love relationship, Josh was exactly the opposite. With Josh there were no pretenses and no guesswork and no surprises. When he was happy, he showed it, and likewise, when he was angry or irritated, he made no attempts to hide it. Everything he said and did was with pure and open honesty; it was simply the way he was—a wonderful, honest, and God-fearing man.

Of course she couldn't help but like him, but love? No. Love took two people, and what Josh felt for her could only be termed as an affable friendship. Therefore, what she returned to him had to be the same.

And that being the case, she had no reasonable explanation of why she was reacting this way in his presence, simply because of a locked door.

She had three choices of where to sit—on the beanbag chair the boys lounged back on when they played their video games, on the office chair at the computer workstation, or on the love seat beside Josh.

He smiled from his side of the love seat and patted the cushion beside him.

Melissa's heart went wild.

Not wanting to give him any idea of what a ninny she was being, she hustled into the empty spot, backing as far into the corner as she could.

She nearly had a heart attack when he reached over and grasped both her hands. His rough, callused hands covered hers completely, and their warmth radiated all the way to her soul.

He smiled, lowered his head, and closed his eyes.

With her heart in her throat, Melissa did the same. During the time Josh took to compose himself and think of his words before he said them aloud, Melissa tried to regain control of her thoughts.

He only wanted to pray, and while she did too, what she wanted more at that moment was not merely for him to hold her hands, she wanted him to hold her—to wrap his arms around her and hold her tight and to whisper sweet nothings in her ear—to kiss her and tell her he loved her.

Melissa squeezed her eyes shut and sucked in a deep breath, completely ashamed of herself.

He gave her hands a gentle squeeze to signify that he was ready. Melissa quickly did her best to wipe all thoughts out of her head except for prayers of agreement as he poured out his heart to God with her as his witness. His words served to deepen the bond that had been growing daily since they'd met.

After his closing "amen" they remained silent, their hands joined, simply gazing into each other's faces. If Josh were the type, and if they had that kind of relationship, Melissa might have called the moment "romantic," if they hadn't just been praying.

At the same time, they heard a shuffle on the other side of the door, followed by whispering.

"They aren't anywhere. They have to be in here."

The doorknob turned very slowly and silently, and Melissa

could see in her mind's eye, a grouping of little boys testing it.

Josh opened his mouth to respond, but before a sound came out of his mouth, the whispering resumed.

"What do you think they're doing? It's awful quiet in there."

"Do you think they're kissing?"

"Kissing? Uncle Josh and Miss Klassen?"

"No, duh. . ."

A chorus of gasps sounded, immediately followed by the scampering away of six little feet.

Josh released her hands as quickly as if she'd burned him and buried his face in his hands. "I don't believe this."

Melissa folded her hands over her chest, hoping the position would stop her hands from shaking. "Come on, Josh, what did you expect? In the kids' eyes, Bradley managed to get us to date, and now, as soon as we decide to taper it off, Ryan pulls that little stunt getting me here to help him with some alleged homework. I'm sure Bradley was in on it too. Can't you see what they're doing?"

"Of course I can see through their little matchmaking attempts. They're not exactly being very subtle."

"Now, according to them, they've succeeded. Instead of showing them that we're going our separate ways, they think we're hiding and, uh, well, you know."

Josh leaned back into his corner of the love seat, stretched his legs out in front of him, and raised his arms, linking his fingers behind his head. Devilment shone from his smiling eyes, and his amused little grin made one dimple appear in his right cheek. "No, Melissa. Tell me. What do they think we're doing?"

She swatted him on the arm and stood. "Stop it. We have to get out of here and show ourselves. I hope that coffee's ready. I think I need it."

❧

Josh walked Melissa to her car, then stood on the curb and waved as she drove away. He couldn't believe the way the evening turned out.

When he heard the kids whispering, asking each other if he was kissing Melissa, instead of a protest, at the time his first thought was that kissing her wasn't such a bad idea.

And that was wrong.

She was Bradley's teacher. Her boss had caught news that they'd been seeing each other, and trouble was on the way if they didn't cease and desist.

He didn't want to cease and desist, but he had to.

Melissa was his friend, probably the most special friend he'd ever had in his whole life.

They understood each other. They could share anything. They could both be at their worst, and they still liked each other, anyway. Best of all, when they were both at their best, they really had fun, and they didn't have to do anything extraordinary or elaborate. One of the most enjoyable nights of his life had happened at the grocery store. He'd always hated grocery shopping, but Melissa had made it fun, at least she had that one night. He hadn't even cared that people stared at them as they walked down the aisles pushing their carts, laughing, and acting silly.

Melissa was everything Bradley said she was and more. He'd never met anyone like her in his whole life, and he never would again.

That was why he couldn't kiss her. Kissing her would change the key focus of their relationship, and he couldn't take the chance that once it changed, they could never go back.

Besides, Melissa had never indicated anything else in their relationship besides pure friendship. If he tried to push her to a point she didn't want to go, he would break her trust. He would rather die than risk doing anything that might damage all they'd come to be to each other.

He found himself still standing on the curb long after her taillights disappeared around the corner. Josh stiffened and walked inside, got the kids ready for bed, then sat down at the computer to e-mail his brother, and following that, Josh would crawl into bed.

Tomorrow was another day.

&

"Josh? What are you doing here? My car is working just fine."

Josh couldn't stop his grin as he held out the plastic grocery bag. "I'm not here about your car. I got a phone call from Tyler just as I was about to leave work. It seems that yesterday you left a bag of groceries in our freezer. You have to realize that food doesn't last long at our house. Tyler phoned, very concerned, to tell me that they ate it all after school, and that I should go to the grocery store on my way home to replace everything immediately."

"They ate all that in one day?"

"Can I come in before this melts?"

Her cheeks turned that charming shade of pink he liked so much as she accepted the bag from him. He followed her into the kitchen and watched as she unpacked the bag and transferred everything into the freezer.

"We go through a can of that frozen juice concentrate in a day, sometimes less. Frozen waffles make a great snack after school. One box lasts approximately fourteen minutes. Bradley opened the frozen asparagus. He wanted to see what it looked like—you know his interest in 'vegabulls.' They cooked it after school, but Tyler said nobody would eat it, by the way. I have a feeling Cleo won't be very hungry for her dinner tonight. I won't mention those ice cream bars you bought. There's only six in a box, and when you gather five boys and one dog, well, we'll just say there isn't anything left for me."

"A long time ago, you made me angry when you said that Cleo was too fat. Now I know why, and I can understand."

"I never said that."

"Yes, you did. Bradley said you said that."

Josh shook his head. He'd learned long ago never to have a battle of words with Melissa, although he'd been known to beat her close to half the time at Scrabble. One time he'd really wiped her because he got the bonus for using all seven letters on the word "chassis."

"Josh?"

"Oops. Sorry. I was thinking about something else."

"I said, the boys obviously know you're here. Are you staying for supper?"

He grinned. "Only if I'm invited." Without waiting for her reply, he sauntered to the stove, lifted the lid to the pot, and peeked inside. "Oh boy! Tuna Noodle Casserole!"

She sighed. "Get yourself a plate."

As he reached into the cupboard to get everything he needed, he turned to speak over his shoulder. "By the way, I've got a change of plans for date night. I have to work some overtime on Saturday, and I know I'm going to be tired so I was going to cancel. Then the kids went and reserved a movie and asked if you'll come and do date night at our house."

"They did, did they?"

He sat at the table to wait for the last few minutes before the timer went off and the casserole was ready. "Have you noticed that when I told them we'd decided to cut back on seeing each other, they created a reason for us to be together every single night of the week?"

"Yes. I also noticed it's not just Bradley anymore, but every single one of them."

They shared a laugh and counted on their fingers for every day recently where each of the boys dreamed up some very sensible and necessary reason to get them together, with the exception of Boys Club and Bible study night. That night, Josh had been so tired he had contemplated not going, when he found them all waiting at the door with their shoes already on and even tied properly.

It didn't take much to convince him to stay and visit for awhile after they'd done the dishes together.

On his way out, he paused and turned around. "See you tomorrow night at our house. Oh, have you got any popcorn? Also, the kids told me to pick the movie up on the way home from work, so come over early, and we'll order pizza for supper."

fourteen

"I think there's been a mistake," Josh said as he handed the movie back to the clerk.

"There's no mistake." The woman pressed her lips together, as if she was trying not to laugh, and gave it to him again. "I remember this. Six boys came in and picked it out, and they even paid for it. Out of their allowances, they told me. It's yours for the weekend. Two-day rental."

Josh felt his face turn ten shades of red. The movie they'd chosen was a weepy chick flick, nothing he would ever have contemplated renting, never mind something a horde of boys would enjoy. Then he remembered Kyle saying that Cody helped them pick it out—the Cody whose mom was dating Erica's dad.

"I guess I'll take it then," he mumbled. "Since it's already paid for."

When he pulled into the driveway, he noticed Melissa's car already parked on the street. He grabbed the movie and hurried inside, but only Cleo greeted him at the door.

He found everyone in the den surrounding Melissa, who was sitting in the kids' bean bag chair with a game controller in her hand. The console had been set to four-player mode, and Melissa was racing as the princess character.

"Remind me never to let you drive my car when I get it out of storage."

"Mmm," she mumbled as she rounded a difficult corner, then spun out over a cliff.

"See what I mean?"

"I give up. I think it's time to order the pizza," she grumbled as she set the controller down.

As soon as Andrew announced his championship at the

finish line, they voted on the pizza toppings. Tyler took over Melissa's player, and Josh took her into the living room, leaving all the boys to continue with their games until supper arrived.

"You won't believe what the kids rented," he said as he pulled the movie out of the bag.

Before he could complain about the schmaltzy story line, Melissa squealed with glee.

"I've been wanting to see this! I heard it's great!"

Josh pasted a very forced smile on his face. "I can hardly wait to see it too." He could hardly wait to see the credits.

As a treat, he allowed everyone to eat the pizza in the living room while they watched the movie, which also acted as a distraction from the feeble characterizations and predictable plot.

Amazingly, all five boys stayed in the living room, politely half watching the movie they'd spent their hard-earned money on, while Melissa's attention remained glued. About halfway through, they paused it for Melissa and Tyler to go into the kitchen to make the popcorn.

The second they left the room, Andrew appeared at Josh's side.

"Aren't you, like, gonna put your arm around Miss Klassen or hold her hand or something, Uncle Josh? Tyler told me that's what guys do when you gotta watch something like this with a girl."

"He did, did he?" Josh decided to supervise Tyler's activities with Allyson a little closer.

"Yeah. That's how you make up for it when nothing gets blown up and there's no racing."

"You think so?"

Andrew grinned. "Not really. But that's what Tyler said to the little kids."

"You got a girlfriend yet, Andrew?"

"No, but Kaitlin always shares her snack with me at junior youth club. I guess that's close."

Another one coming up who would soon need more supervision. Josh wondered if he had bitten off more than he could chew.

"Popcorn, everyone! Let's turn the movie back on."

"Hold on. Let's get these pizza boxes out of here first. And get rid of these empty drink cans."

When all the boys hustled into the kitchen, Josh stepped up to Melissa.

"Andrew asked me why I haven't put my arm around you or something."

"Pardon me?"

"That's why they rented this particular movie. They're expecting to see some romance happening."

She glanced at the doorway leading to the kitchen, where the noise level indicated they were all ready to return. "They think we were kissing the other day when we locked the door to the den. Isn't that enough?"

"Apparently it only encouraged them."

"What do you think we should do?"

"Maybe we should start acting a little more like we're really dating in front of them. I think the reason they're doing this is they thought we were going to split up. Let's show them we're not about to split up, and they'll leave us alone."

"Okay. . ."

Before Josh could comment further, the boys stampeded back to their spots.

After he flipped the movie back on, just as they'd agreed, he slipped his arm around Melissa. At first she stiffened, which made him wonder if he'd done it wrong, but after a few minutes, she relaxed and started to lean a little into him.

Josh smiled. He liked it. It wasn't exactly kissing her, but under the circumstances, he figured it was the next best thing.

As the movie continued, the aroma of the popcorn and the sound of munching all around started getting to him. He was the only one not eating any, because he was the only one with one arm otherwise occupied and therefore without a bowl.

With his free hand he reached for a handful of popcorn from the bowl in Melissa's lap. The action caused him to turn slightly, which in turn caused him to lean into her as she leaned into him.

The motion brought his face very close to hers.

He shoved the entire handful of popcorn into his mouth at once, leaned his face a little closer, and grinned like a squirrel with its cheeks stuffed full of nuts.

She turned to face him, one cheek bulging slightly from her smaller nibbles of popcorn. She froze, midchew. "What are you doing?" she mumbled around her mouthful.

When she turned, it brought her face close to his, barely a couple of inches apart. Close enough to kiss her. Except they both had their faces stuffed with popcorn, and they shared a room with five kids.

"I'm trying to be romantic," he tried to whisper clearly through the popcorn puffing out both cheeks. "Is it working?"

"Stop it, and pay attention to the movie."

Reluctantly, he turned back to the television, but studying Melissa interested him far more than the dumb movie.

He could feel her whole body stiffen at the tense moments and sag at the slow parts. At one romantic moment, she snuggled into him even more. Between the movie and holding her, he wanted to respond.

Again, he reached into the bowl in her lap, but this time when he leaned into her, he turned his head all the way and brushed her hair with his lips.

"Stop it," she whispered without turning. "The kids."

He grinned and nuzzled further into her hair and brushed a quick kiss on her ear. "I thought this was the whole idea. Besides, they're all glued to the television. It's finally a racing scene. If they're lucky, the car will blow up."

"Then turn around and watch it, and maybe you'll get lucky too."

Josh grinned and leaned closer to her ear. "Nothing, nothing," he whispered.

She turned her head so fast he didn't have a chance to move. Again, her mouth was so close to his that he could have kissed her. But this time he didn't have his mouth stuffed full of pop-corn. He really could have, if the kids weren't in the room.

"What are you doing?" she ground out in a harsh whisper.

He felt his grin falter at where his thoughts were turning. "I was whispering sweet nothings in your ear."

Her mouth dropped open, but no words came out. Abruptly, she tilted her head away and turned her face back to the televi-sion. "I don't know what you think you're doing, but quit it."

Reluctantly, he turned back to the movie, but he couldn't concentrate on the action on the screen. He could only think of the woman in his arms.

If he had thought he could keep their relationship to a pla-tonic friendship, he now realized he had only been deluding himself. He'd been very careful not to touch her in any way since they first began their convoluted friendship, and this was exactly the reason why. He'd crossed the line, and he couldn't go back. He wanted to deepen the relationship. He not only wanted to kiss her now, but he wanted to kiss her every time he said hello, every time he said good-bye, plus a little in between.

Except he didn't have that right. The circumstances of his life did not allow for the time or energy to participate in a two-sided relationship. He had nothing to offer her past his friendship on days it was convenient for him, and a few kisses, which would have been entirely for his benefit. Not only that, she still had her job to deal with. A friendship based on helping one of her students she could defend. She couldn't defend a blossoming romance with a student's guardian because that was exactly what her principal was pressuring her into abstaining from.

Just because her boss was wrong and had no jurisdiction to interfere with her personal life didn't change the fact that it was happening. He didn't want to encourage her to get the teacher's union to do battle for him when it was a dead issue before it started. He simply couldn't have that kind of relationship with her anyway.

All he could do was continue to hold her through the movie, which was approaching the pivotal moment and therefore the end. Suddenly, he didn't want the movie to end. He wanted it to last at least another hour, because when it ended, he would have to let her go.

He strengthened his grasp around her shoulder when her body made a slight jerk. He wondered if he'd maybe squeezed her too tight because of the million conflicting thoughts cascading through his brain, but then she turned to him.

Out of the corner of his eye, he noticed the credits rolling down the screen. A few tears dribbled down her cheeks, and she smiled at him. The combination punched a hole in his heart that he knew would never heal.

"That was so good," she sniffled. "Thanks for inviting me."

Josh froze. He wanted to kiss those tears away, then hold her and kiss her just because he wanted to. He didn't know what to do.

"Miss Klassen? Why are you crying? The movie had a happy ending. Nothing got blowed up."

Melissa backed up, forcing Josh to let his arm drop to his side. She wiped her tears away with the back of her hand. "Sometimes girls cry at happy endings, Ryan," she sniffled. "That was a very good movie."

"Really?"

Josh cleared his throat to get everyone's attention. "Everybody pick up your popcorn bowls before Cleo gets into them, and put them on the counter, not on the table where she can get them. Then you can go play video games until bed. But only if you're quiet."

Melissa checked her watch as the boys diligently picked up the bowls and filed into the kitchen. "I know it's still fairly early, but I should be going. I have a Sunday school teacher's meeting before the service starts tomorrow morning, and I have to get up early. I'll see you all at church tomorrow."

"I'll see you to your car. This feels so strange, me seeing

you out. This isn't the way a date is supposed to end."

"Don't worry about it," she said as he escorted her outside. "I had a nice evening, and that's what's important."

Melissa unlocked her car door and opened it, but before she got in, Josh gently touched her on the shoulder and turned her to face him.

He stepped closer. "This is the way a date is supposed to end." He rested one hand at the side of her waist and trailed the fingers of his other hand down the soft skin of her cheek, stopping when his index finger reached the bottom of her dainty little chin.

Slowly, he tipped her chin up and slid his other hand around her back.

"Josh? What are you doing? I saw the blinds move. The boys are watching."

"The boys can mind their own business for a change."

Without waiting for her response, he lowered his head, closed his eyes, and claimed her mouth, kissing her with all the love in his heart. She stiffened for a brief second, relaxed, and then kissed him back the same way he was kissing her.

Slowly, he could feel her fingers at his waist, then her hands flattened against him and slid around his back.

His heart pounded. He might have died and gone to heaven, except he was still breathing. Actually, he wasn't breathing.

Josh released her mouth and told himself to breathe, but he didn't release his embrace. Gradually he opened his eyes to see Melissa's shimmering eyes staring right back at him, and her lips showed the trace of a slight smile.

He couldn't stand it. He didn't care if the boys or half the neighborhood was watching. Josh only cared about the woman in his arms. The woman he loved.

He tilted his head slightly and kissed her again. All the emptiness in his soul filled to overflowing. He felt contentment and excitement at the same time. Kissing Melissa was like shooting stars.

Like. . .

fifteen

Fireworks!

Ever since the kids had caught them in the den behind the locked door, Melissa had wondered what it would be like if Josh ever kissed her. She'd dreamed about it.

Her dreams paled in comparison to the reality of his kiss and his tender embrace.

Very slowly, his mouth released hers. Instead of letting her go, his fingers threaded into her hair and guided her head to rest against his chest while he continued to hold her tightly, almost desperately, like he didn't want to let her go. She could almost feel the frantic beating of his heart against her cheek, because she could certainly hear it.

Melissa knew her own was no different. She also knew that in the last minute, everything had changed, and her life would never be the same again.

Josh lowered his face into her hair and pressed his cheek into her temple, completing his embrace from head to toe.

"Wow," he said, his voice echoing strangely in his chest with her ear pressed against it. "I never knew."

"Me neither."

"What are we going to do?" he whispered huskily.

"I don't know."

The only thing she did know was that she had to go home. She couldn't think properly with Josh wrapped around her. Never mind think properly—she couldn't think at all.

"Will you come over for lunch after church? I think we have to talk."

"Yes," she said as she backed up a step, forcing him to drop his arms and lift his head.

Before she could contemplate if she should kiss him

good-bye after all that, she hustled into the car, shut the door, and drove off. She had a lot to think about before tomorrow. And a lot of praying to do.

✍

Melissa stopped to think, her arms immersed nearly up to her elbows in the sudsy water, halfway in the middle of scrubbing the cooked-on eggs from the bottom of the pan. Having such a serious conversation while doing dishes may have been rather bizarre, but she needed the distraction.

They both did.

"So we're agreed, then?"

Melissa nodded. "Yes."

Josh stuffed the dish towel over the handle for the oven door, stared at it, then yanked it off and handed it to her. "Leave that. Let's go talk to the boys and get it over with."

She sat on the recliner to wait for Josh to get the boys from the den, not because she liked the chair, but because it was the only single chair in the room. She didn't want anyone to sit beside her today, not even Josh.

Josh sat all the boys down. "We have to talk to you guys."

Everyone became deathly silent.

"Miss Klassen and I know what you guys have been doing. You've been pretty good, but we've known almost from the beginning about all these little matchmaking schemes."

If her stomach wasn't churning so badly, and if she wasn't on the verge of a major stress headache, Melissa would have laughed at their instantly red faces and mouths dropping open. They alternated between staring at the floor and studying some unknown blank space on the wall.

"What we're going to tell you now is that we've decided to stop pretending to be dating for you guys. Miss Klassen and I are just friends, and we'll always be just friends. We weren't dating, and we never were."

"But you went out on lots of dates! We know you did!"

"We were together, but it wasn't real dating. Most of the time we just stayed at Miss Klassen's house and talked and stuff. Sometimes we did grocery shopping. Sometimes I helped her with school stuff. Lots of times I was so tired all I did was lay on the couch and have a nap while Miss Klassen did her housework."

Josh stopped talking, probably to let the magnitude of what he said sink in. Not one of them said a word.

"Most of all, we're not going to date for real because neither one of us is in a position to do that."

Kyle blinked repeatedly and squirmed in his chair.

Josh nodded at him. "Yes, Kyle?"

"Why not?"

"Because it's not fair. Dating is a special kind of relationship that takes a lot of things that I just can't do right now. You know what it's like when you do something with a partner at school, and you get stuck doing all the hard stuff, and the other kid does nothing?"

All five boys nodded in unison.

"When you go out with a girl, it's kind of the same thing. Two people have to put in equal shares of the work as well as the fun stuff, or it's not fair. You understand about being fair?"

They all nodded again.

Melissa thought Josh explained things very well. He'd only left out the reason that he couldn't commit to a two-sided relationship, and that was something he couldn't say. It was because of his responsibilities to his brother and sister-in-law in raising the boys and being the head of their household until Brian and Sasha returned.

If it wasn't for the boys, they could have dated for real. But then again, if it wasn't for the boys, he would be engaged or possibly even married to Theresa by now. Either way, she couldn't have him. It was only because of the boys that she'd met him at all, and for the short space of her life that she had him, she had to be thankful.

"Miss Klassen also has something to say to you."

All eyes turned to her.

"There's another reason I can't date your uncle Josh for real, and it's very complicated. At the school there is a rule that a teacher isn't allowed to date anyone who has kids in their class. That's for two reasons, but only one is really important to you. Do you understand the meaning of the word 'favoritism'?"

Tyler and Andrew nodded, but the other three stared at her blankly.

Finally Ryan spoke. "Is that like having a favorite toy?"

"In a way, but it's different with people. Think of your favorite toy."

The three younger boys nodded. She wasn't exactly sure about Andrew, but she knew Tyler already understood what she was going to say.

"When you have a favorite toy, you treat it special. It's kind of the same with people, but a teacher can't have a favorite student because that wouldn't be fair to the other students, to treat one better than the rest."

Bradley thrust his hand in the air, as if he was in the classroom instead of his own living room. "But I know you'd never do that. I don't have to be your favorite student if you do dating with Uncle Josh."

"That's only part of it, Bradley. Even if I didn't show any favoritism, there would be other kids who would say I treated you better, even if it weren't true. And that causes problems in the class. There's only one way to stop that from happening, and that's not to do dating with anyone in a student's family."

Bradley's eyes filled with tears. "Then I can change classes. I can move into Miss Henry's class. I don't want no fabratizm."

"There's nothing you can do about it, Bradley. It's just one of those unfair things in life that happens and there's nothing you can do about it."

Tyler's voice came out in a rather low rumble for a fifteen year old. "Does that mean you and Uncle Josh are splitting up?"

Melissa cleared her throat. "Tyler, we were never together. We only pretended to be, in order to make everyone feel better. We can't pretend anymore. Okay?"

"I guess. . ."

Rather than prolong the agony, Melissa stood. "I have to go now. Don't worry, Uncle Josh and I are still friends. We always will be. Right, Uncle Josh?"

Josh also stood. "Right, Miss Klassen."

Briefly she glanced at him. Unless it was her imagination Josh's voice sounded a bit strange, but she couldn't put her finger on it.

"I'll see you at school tomorrow, Bradley. Good-bye."

And with those words, Melissa did the hardest thing she'd ever done in her life.

She walked out of the McMillian house, knowing she could never go back.

❧

Josh sat at the kitchen table, staring at the clock, watching the second hand move in its circular path with jerky little movements, the checkbook in front of him not any more balanced than it had been an hour ago.

Numbly, he laid the pen on the table and buried his face in his hands.

He blew it. He'd never blown anything so bad in his entire life. He knew before he kissed her that once he did it, he could never go back. He'd kissed her anyway, and now, it was too late. She was gone from his life, and it was all his fault.

When Theresa left him, he didn't miss her. Instead it had left him feeling stupid and manipulated that he hadn't seen her selfishness for the entire time he'd known her.

He'd soon put thoughts of Theresa aside, but he thought of Melissa night and day. He may have been fooling himself into thinking they could only be platonic friends, but he'd managed to make it last for awhile before he'd stepped over the line. Even though their relationship was as one-sided as he vowed it would never be, the loss of her friendship and everything that went with it felt like a piece of him had been ripped apart, stomped on by a herd of buffalo, and flushed down the toilet.

Even the boys had been affected.

They hadn't had a fight in a week.

Their rooms were all picked up.

Their homework was done. On time. Every day.

Josh had never been so miserable in his life.

&

"Class dismissed. Please tuck your chairs in neatly, and proceed quietly to the back for your coats."

Melissa didn't have the energy or the desire to stand at the back and smile and parrot cheerful platitudes. Today she simply remained at her desk at the front and watched the children file out.

Instead of going to the back with his classmates, a somber Bradley appeared in front of her desk.

"Yes, Bradley?"

"I thought you said that you were still going to be friends with Uncle Josh."

For a second, Melissa's heart stopped, then pounded in her chest. "We're still friends, Bradley." However, for a while, until she could get used to the gaping wound in her heart from missing him, she couldn't see him or talk to him. Every time she did, it would feel like she would be again ripped in two.

"Then why is Uncle Josh so sad all the time?"

The back of her throat tightened, and the backs of her eyes burned, but she managed to control herself. She didn't want to cry in front of Bradley. She'd shed enough tears from missing Josh to last a lifetime, and it had been just a little over a week.

"I don't know why he's sad, Bradley. Shouldn't you be going to Darlene's house? She'll be worried if you're late."

"I'm not getting baby-sat today. Uncle Josh is home, and I have to go home to look after him."

Melissa's hand froze, and the pen skidded a red line across the paper she had been marking. "What do you mean, look after him?"

"Uncle Josh was barfing his guts out in the middle of the night, and he tried to go to work this morning, but he had to run back to the bathroom to barf up some more. He never went to work. He had to stay home all day all by himself." Bradley's eyes opened wide and he frowned, like he thought that was a bad thing. "Me and Kyle and Ryan gotta look after him until Andrew and Tyler get home."

Melissa didn't know if having the three youngest boys attempting to care for Josh while he was down with the flu would make things better or worse.

It didn't take a lot of imagination for her to picture Josh trying to look after all the kids, even sick.

"Come on, Bradley. I'll give you a ride home. Have your brothers left yet?"

She found Ryan and Kyle waiting for Bradley outside the classroom door, so she hurried them to her car and drove as quickly as she could to their house without getting a speeding ticket.

The door wasn't locked. She ran in and found Josh lying on the bathroom floor. She could only imagine what it cost him to go unlock the front door so the kids could get in.

"What are you doing here?" he groaned.

Melissa dropped to her knees. "You're burning with fever. Let me get you to bed."

"Can't leave the bathroom."

"I doubt you have anything left in your system. Have you been drinking any water? You don't want to get dehydrated."

"No," he groaned.

"Kyle," she called out over her shoulder, knowing the three boys were standing in the hall, watching through the open bathroom doorway. "Go downstairs and get the bucket, and put it beside Uncle Josh's bed. Ryan, pour your uncle a glass of water, not too cold."

She turned to Josh and wrapped her hands around one of his arms. "You belong in bed, not on the floor."

Melissa guided him to bed, and when Kyle returned with the bucket, she went for a wet face cloth to cool his forehead. "Have you been like this all day?" she asked as she dug a couple of headache tablets out of her purse. "Take these, they'll help with the fever. And if they don't stay down, that's what the bucket is for."

"My mother used to do this for me," he mumbled as he sipped the water with the pills, then collapsed back onto the bed. "I don't want you to see me like this. I'll be fine."

"Right. You look fine."

He didn't comment further, so she simply sat on the edge of the bed and watched him lie there, unmoving.

She prepared herself for him to protest about her staying, but he remained silent, which was good. She didn't want another self-sacrificing speech from him about how it was wrong for him not to put anything into their relationship. She'd been thinking about everything he said for over a week, and the more she thought about it, the more she disagreed with his conclusion.

It wasn't his fault he needed to put everything he had into the boys first and foremost. What he was doing was good and right, and she loved him even more for it. For now, if he had to pay more attention to his nephews than her, she didn't care.

Gently, she rested the backs of her fingers against his un-shaved cheek. "You're not as hot as you were fifteen minutes ago. I think those pills are starting to work. Bradley said you were up all night. Have you slept at all today?"

"No."

"The water is staying down. Want to try some juice?"

"I dunno."

In the background, Cleo barked, and then the front door slammed. Within a minute, Andrew appeared in the doorway. "Uncle Josh, are you feeling bett. . . ?" His voice trailed off. "Oh. Hi, Miss Klassen. Is Uncle Josh better?"

"Not yet, Andrew. Can you go get him a half a glass of juice?"

"Yeah, sure."

Before Andrew returned, Cleo barked, and the door slammed again.

"Uncle Josh?" Tyler hollered. "Is that—" Tyler appeared in the doorway. "Miss Klassen's car in the—Oh, hi, Miss Klassen. Is Uncle Josh better?"

Andrew appeared behind Tyler, holding a glass.

"Not yet, Tyler," she said.

She helped Josh lean up while he swallowed one small sip of juice, then sank back down. "I can't drink that. You can go. The kids are all home now."

"No. I'm staying. And I want to stay around for a long time. Not just until you're better. I want to stay with you forever."

He turned his head to the side and froze for a second, making Melissa wonder if she should make a grab for the bucket. His eyes focused somewhere behind her. "Don't you two have someplace else to go?"

Melissa turned around just in time to see Andrew and Tyler disappear through the doorway.

His focus returned to her face. "What do you mean, forever? You're talking to a guy with five kids to look after. If you want to do forever, you'll have to be prepared that by the time you get really attached to the kids, their parents will come back and we'll lose them, and then we'd have to go find and live in some empty, quiet apartment."

"I have a duplex. I could rent it out until we needed it. And nothing would stop us from visiting the boys often, or the boys from coming to visit with us either."

He winced, rolled to his side, drew his knees up a little, covered his stomach with one hand, and closed his eyes.

"Poor baby," Melissa whispered, and covered him with the blanket.

After the wave of nausea passed, he opened one eye. "About this forever stuff. I've been thinking about that thing with your principal. It won't be that long before Bradley is out of grade one, so this problem is temporary." Both eyes opened, but she could see that the exhaustion was finally starting to claim him. "We could invite him to the wedding, and if he doesn't come, report him to the union. That is, if you really would marry a guy with all this extra baggage."

Melissa ran her fingers through his hair and brushed a stray lock off his forehead. "I would in a minute. If that guy asked me."

He looked up at her, and the combination between his pale and drawn face and the circles under his glassy eyes nearly brought her to tears.

He made a short cough and shivered. "This isn't right. Can I propose properly tomorrow?"

Melissa smiled. "You'd better. I'm going to go make supper for your family. Promise me you won't go anywhere."

A weak smile flittered across his face for a brief second, and his eyes closed. "I love you, Miss Klassen," he murmured, and his breathing became shallow and even.

"I love you too, Uncle Josh," she whispered and tucked the blanket under his chin.

The bedsprings creaked as Melissa stood. Before she took her first step, from the hall she heard a whispered "yippee!" as ten feet and four paws scampered away.

A Letter To Our Readers

Dear Reader:

In order that we might better contribute to your reading enjoyment, we would appreciate your taking a few minutes to respond to the following questions. We welcome your comments and read each form and letter we receive. When completed, please return to the following:

Rebecca Germany, Fiction Editor
Heartsong Presents
PO Box 719
Uhrichsville, Ohio 44683

1. Did you enjoy reading *McMillian's Matchmakers* by Gail Sattler?

   ❏ Very much! I would like to see more books by this author!

   ❏ Moderately. I would have enjoyed it more if

   _____

   _____

2. Are you a member of **Heartsong Presents**? Yes ❏ No ❏
   If no, where did you purchase this book?_____

   _____

3. How would you rate, on a scale from 1 (poor) to 5 (superior), the cover design?_____

4. On a scale from 1 (poor) to 10 (superior), please rate the following elements.

   _____ Heroine   _____ Plot

   _____ Hero   _____ Inspirational theme

   _____ Setting   _____ Secondary characters

5. These characters were special because_____

_____

_____

6. How has this book inspired your life?_____

_____

_____

7. What settings would you like to see covered in future **Heartsong Presents** books?_____

_____

_____

8. What are some inspirational themes you would like to see treated in future books?_____

_____

_____

9. Would you be interested in reading other **Heartsong Presents** titles?   Yes ❏   No ❏

10. Please check your age range:
   ❏ Under 18   ❏ 18-24   ❏ 25-34
   ❏ 35-45   ❏ 46-55   ❏ Over 55

Name _____

Occupation _____

Address _____

City _____ State _____ Zip _____

Email _____

NEW ENGLAND

NEW ENGLAND

From the majestic mountains to the glorious seashore, experience the beauty New England offers the romantic heart. Four respected authors will take you on an unforgettable trip with true-to-life characters.

Here's your ticket for a refreshing escape to the Northeast. Enjoy the view as God works His will in the lives of those who put their trust in Him.

paperback, 476 pages, 5 ¾6" x 8"

❤ · ❤ · ❤ · ❤ · ❤ · ❤ · ❤ · ❤ · ❤ · ❤ · ❤ · ❤ · ❤ · ❤

❤ · ❤ · ❤ · ❤ · ❤ · ❤ · ❤ · ❤ · ❤ · ❤ · ❤ · ❤ · ❤ · ❤

·······Presents·······

Hearts♥ng Presents
Love Stories Are Rated G!

That's for godly, gratifying, and of course, great! If you love a thrilling love story but don't appreciate the sordidness of some popular paperback romances, **Heartsong Presents** is for you. In fact, **Heartsong Presents** is the *only inspirational romance book club* featuring love stories where Christian faith is the primary ingredient in a marriage relationship.

Sign up today to receive your first set of four never-before-published Christian romances. Send no money now; you will receive a bill with the first shipment. You may cancel at any time without obligation, and if you aren't completely satisfied with any selection, you may return the books for an immediate refund!

Imagine. . .four new romances every four weeks—two historical, two contemporary—with men and women like you who long to meet the one God has chosen as the love of their lives. . .all for the low price of $9.97 postpaid.

To join, simply complete the coupon below and mail to the address provided. **Heartsong Presents** romances are rated G for another reason: They'll arrive *Godspeed!*